LAVINA'S CHRISTMAS MIRACLE

AN AMISH ROMANCE

Naomi Troyer

Contents

Chapter 1 A List of Unachievables 3

Chapter 2 A Quick Escape...8

Chapter 3 A Child's Honesty 12

Chapter 4 Poverty Isn't a Sin 16

Chapter 5 The Gift of Christmas 21

Chapter 6 A Stranger Comes Calling..24

Chapter 7 A Delightful Dinner..29

Chapter 8 Honest Confessions...33

Chapter 9 Chicken Coop Catastrophe...38

Chapter 10 The Negotiations Begin...42

Chapter 11 A Fair Trade...46

Chapter 12 Blackmail & Buggy Rides 50

Chapter 13 A Schweschder's Concern 57

Chapter 14 The Lord Repays Graciousness to the Poor........61

Chapter 15 Arranging Priorities 65

Chapter 16 An Unwelcome Visit...71

Chapter 17 Selling Dreams 76

Chapter 18 Their Mysterious Christmas Angel 81

Chapter 19 Hochmuth is a Sin 87

Chapter 20 A Flavor for Every Schweschder........................91

Chapter 21 Cocoa and Promises...97

Chapter 22 A Romance Unfolds...101

Epilogue 106

Chapter 1
A List of Unachievables

"Here's the list."

"Denke," Lavina Schrock accepted the piece of paper from her younger sister and scanned over the items they needed. She suppressed a sigh, knowing that there was no way they could afford to purchase everything they needed.

"Lavina?" Johanna asked quietly beside her.

Lavina turned to her sister, only two years her junior and shook her head. As the eldest of five sisters, it was Lavina's responsibility to care for her family ever since her mother had passed away in August.

Lavina was the oldest at twenty-four. Johanna was twenty-two and next came Elizabeth at nineteen. Bonny and Daisy were the youngest. Bonny just finished the eighth grade this year and celebrated her fourteenth birthday a month ago. Then there was Daisy, only ten years old.

It broke Lavina's heart to know that Daisy had lost her mother at such a young age. Just like it broke her heart to come into town with her sisters, knowing they wouldn't be able to afford the items that they need.

"Let me just see how much we have." Lavina said, opening her purse. She counted the bills and coins—they'll need every penny.

"Look, Christmas trees!" Daisy cried out with excitement.

"Hush Daisy, Lavina is thinking," Johanna quickly quieted their youngest sister before turning to Lavina. "And?"

"Schweschders, I'm afraid to say we won't be able to get everything we need. We'll prioritize and make do with what can buy." Lavina summoned a smile. "We each get to pick an item on the list and from there we'll see what else we can afford."

"Soap," Johanna was the first to answer.

"Flour," Bonny announced. As the baker in the family, Lavina had expected nothing less.

"Pasta," Elizabeth said just as Daisy announced her item.

"Cocoa."

"Right," Lavina looked at the list and sighed. "That means I take toilet paper."

The sound of her sisters laughing lightened her heart just a little, but not enough to give her hope for what tomorrow might bring.

Ever since her mother had passed, Lavina had been struggling to get them back on their feet. Lavina's income from quilts and crochet work had always been enough along with Johanna's income from working at the local farm stall. But their mother's illness had resulted in too many medical bills to count. Most of them they had already paid off, which meant they were living hand to mouth at the moment. Every quilt Lavina sold and every shift Johanna worked, earned them only enough to get by for a few more days.

At the moment, Lavina simply couldn't see a way out of the dark hole of debt they found themselves in. They only had a few more bills to pay, then they'd hopefully be in the clear by end of January, but until then it was going to be tight.

If it were any other time of the year, Lavina wouldn't have felt bad about tightening their belts, but Christmas was only a few weeks away. Johanna was falling short on shifts at the farm stall because they would close for two weeks over the holidays, and as for selling quilts, Lavina couldn't seem to quilt fast enough to make ends meet.

For their family Christmas had always been the most wonderful time of the year. They would put up a tree in the living room, decorate the house with candles and homemade decorations, and they would each secretly make home-made gifts for each other. On Christmas day everyone would band together to cook up a feast to celebrate the occasion.

Then there were all the traditions leading up to Christmas. Each tradition cost money, money that Lavina simply didn't have at the moment. How could they spend a day baking cookies, when they needed the flour and the sugar to last until after Christmas? How could she afford the paper, string, and paint they needed to make new bunting?

As they walked into the store, Lavina couldn't help but notice how expensive everything was, especially when you didn't have the money to buy it.

Daisy stopped in the candy aisle with hopeful eyes. "Lavina, can we have some candy?"

Before Lavina could answer, Johanna took Daisy's hand. "Not today, flower girl. Maybe next time."

Lavina smiled at Johanna's pet name for Daisy. They might not have a lot of money, but at least she knew they had an abundance of love in their family. This Christmas she just needed to make her sisters, especially the younger ones, realize that although they wouldn't have all the traditions, at least they had each other.

Meticulously, she walked through the aisles, ticking off items on her list. Some choices were harder than others. It was easy to choose between salt and the other spices she had on her list, salt was paramount with cooking and baking.

But then there were other choices that weren't as easy. Lavina stood in front of the meat and let out a sigh. She needed to choose between ground beef that could serve them for at least three meals if she stretched it, or cheese.

Cheese had always been a staple in their home, but today, Lavina simply couldn't afford it.

"We're not getting the cheese?" Bonny asked, horrified when Lavina scratched it off her list.

"Maybe next time," Lavina sighed quietly. She hated having to make these decisions. She had always enjoyed being the eldest, now it simply wasn't as rewarding.

Instead, every decision fell to her. It was her responsibility to keep her sisters safe, warm, and fed over the holidays. A task she found to be challenging. They had enough wood to last them through the winter, but the wood still needed to be split. It was an arduous task, especially in the cold, but one that Lavina already knew would fall to her.

By the time they reached the checkout point, Lavina glanced at the few items in their basket. It wasn't even half of what they had on their list, and she wasn't even sure she'd have enough money to pay for it.

She bit back the tears that burned her eyes, realizing they wouldn't solve her problem. It would only be another couple of months and they would be back on their feet, but right now, Lavina felt as if she were on her knees.

Chapter 2
A Quick Escape

Johanna and Elizabeth carried their purchases out of the grocer, while Lavina made sure the two little ones stayed close. It was a busy morning in town. Lavina couldn't help but notice the Englischers on the street carrying purchases that were most probably Christmas gifts. She could never understand why Englischers spent so much money on gifts that were mostly unnecessary and would never be used.

Their family tradition of making homemade gifts carried a lot more sentiment and were often items that could be used. She spotted a family across the road, a mother, father and their two children. Her heart clenched in her chest, wishing she could go back to the time when their family was whole.

Lavina still had vivid memories of her father, but she knew that Daisy and Bonny probably didn't remember him at all. He had passed away nine years ago in a buggy accident; Daisy had only been a few months old and Bonny had barely turned five.

It had been a difficult time for their family, but Lavina would always remember the pillar of strength her mother had been for them. That was what she needed to be now, but she couldn't help but doubt if she was strong enough.

The father scooped his daughter onto his shoulders, making the little girl laugh with glee as the mother and son joined in the laughter. Lavina was captivated by the moment, she didn't even see Daisy rush off until it was too late.

Daisy dashed away from them, disappearing through the people on the sidewalk.

"Daisy!" Lavina cried out as she ran after her youngest sister.

She heard Johanna and Elizabeth rush after her as they called to Bonny to stay close. Lavina made her way through the people with constant excuses until she spotted Daisy standing by the tree lot.

A wave of relief washed over her until a flood of guilt replaced it. Daisy stood in front of a large Christmas tree, admiring it with wide eyes.

"Lavina, look how pretty this one is," Daisy smiled brightly as Lavina reached her.

"It is real pretty, Daisy. Kumm, we need to get going," Lavina said quietly, this wasn't the place or the time to remind her youngest sister that they simply couldn't afford one this year.

"Hullo," a young Amish man said, moving towards them. "How can I help you today? In the market for a Douglas Fir?"

Lavina shook her head and summoned a smile. "Nee, nee. My schweschder was just looking at the trees."

Lavina bent over and whispered in Daisy's ear. "Daisy, kumm!"

"I have a wide variety, from small to huge, all for a great price." The man smiled at them eagerly before he ran through the prices of the different sizes of trees.

"Not today, denke," Lavina said, reaching for Daisy's hand. "Daisy," she warned quietly.

Daisy pulled free from her grip and stepped closer to the tree. She wrapped her arms around it as if it were a giant bear and drew in a deep breath. "Smell it, Lavina. It smells like Christmas."

"Imagine if your entire house was filled with that scent," the man said encouraging Daisy, who didn't need any encouragement at all.

"Daisy!" Lavina said firmly. "The schweschders are waiting for us."

"It won't take but a minute for me to get this one wrapped up for you and loaded onto your buggy."

Lavina smiled stiffly at the man, "Not today."

Daisy shook her head at Lavina and turned to the man selling the Christmas trees. "She's not being rude, we just don't really have any money," Daisy shrugged as if revealing their financial situation to a complete stranger was perfectly normal.

Lavina winced, hoping the man would give up and let them go.

"I'm real sorry to hear that," he sympathized, kneeling down in front of Daisy.

"It's all right. We're not usually poor but after Mamm died, Lavina said we needed to tighten our belts because of the medical bills. I don't really understand what that means because I don't wear belts. I wear dresses," Daisy explained eagerly.

Lavina wanted to wrap a hand over Daisy's mouth to stop her from talking, but her youngest schweschder just kept babbling.

"That's why we can't have a tree this Christmas. We're not even going to bake cookies. We have to make hard choices, Lavina says. Like just now, we had to choose between ground beef and cheese. Lavina chose to ground beef, but I like cheese more."

"Daisy!" Lavina chastened her sister firmly. "That's enough."

Daisy turned to Lavina with a frown. "You said it's nothing to be ashamed of, so why are you angry?" Daisy turned back to the stranger. "That's why I came to look at your trees. We can't have one this year, but I thought if I just came over and smelled it real gut, I'll remember the scent on Christmas day. That way I can imagine we have a tree, even if we don't."

Lavina shot her eyes to the heavens above even as she clenched her jaw. She had never believed in scolding children for their honest naivety, but after what Daisy was doing now, a good scolding was going to be the least of her problems.

Chapter 3
A Child's Honesty

Eli Smucker couldn't help but be enchanted by the little girl's honesty.

She had shared so much information in just a few sentences he wasn't sure to which revelation he should react first. That they had lost their mother, or that they were paying medical bills causing them to have a rough time.

Or should he respond to the little girl's idea of smelling the Douglas Fir and recalling the scent on Christmas day?

As the little girl jabbered on about not being able to paint bunting or buy a ham for Christmas day, Eli sympathized with her older sister. Her sister's revelations clearly humiliated her, trying very hard to hide both her shame and embarrassment, although her cheeks were flushed bright red.

She was beautiful in a quiet sort of way. At first glance you wouldn't notice anything special about her, but the more you looked the more you noticed how uniquely pretty she was. The shape of her eyes made them look big, like pools of glass looking back at him. Her skin was smooth without even the merest hint of a freckle in sight. Her hair, that he could only see a little piece of beneath her prayer kapp, reminded him of the color of honey.

"Can I come and give this tree a hug if we come to town again?" the little girl finally asked, interrupting his thoughts.

Eli smiled. "Of course you may."

For Eli's family, Christmas was just as a special time of the year as it seemed to be for the little girl and her family. During the warmer months his family farmed corn, but throughout the year they grew Douglas Firs to sell over Christmas.

Eli enjoyed setting up the tree lot on Main Street every November. Not only did he get to talk to people from all different backgrounds, but he got to see the joy on their faces when they took home their Christmas tree. For Eli, a Christmas tree was the most important part of Christmas. The scent could fill your home within hours, leaving no doubt what season it was.

For him, it was a privilege to bring that joy to families all over town and the communities beyond.

He searched the older sister's face and tried to remember if he'd seen her before. Three Amish communities surrounded their small town, and Eli knew for a fact that she didn't belong to his congregation. He would've remembered if he'd seen her before. A beauty like hers wasn't something you'd easily forget.

"Daisy, that's enough. Kumm, now!" the oldest sister said firmly.

The little girl sighed and shook her head. "You know, Lavina, it doesn't cost money to look at a tree."

Lavina, now that Eli knew her name, flushed even a brighter shade of red. Before she could scold her sister for back talking, Eli stepped in.

"I haven't seen you around before. In which community do you live?" Eli asked the little girl, knowing she would answer without hesitation.

"The one on the other side of town. Bishop Hauptfleisch's congregation. He's the one that did the service for Mamm's funeral," she informed him with a nod of her head.

"Ah, I see," Eli said with a smile. And how does one get to your haus?"

"It's really easy to see," Daisy began with a look of concentration. "When you drive out of town, you go left at the first tree…"

"Daisy, he doesn't really want to know," Lavina cautioned, taking her sister's hand.

"But he asked," Daisy argued before she turned back to Eli. "Then you follow the dirt road past the red barn and the pond and our haus will be on your right. It's blue, the color of the sky."

"I can imagine it's beautiful," Eli said with a smile.

"It is," Daisy nodded.

"I'm really sorry about this, she gets lost in the moment and then…" Lavina explained.

Eli held up his hand with a kind smile. "There's nothing to apologize for, she's adorable. I'm Eli, by the way. Eli Smucker. I take it you're Lavina and she's Daisy?"

"Jah, now if you'll excuse us, our schweschders are waiting by the buggy. Daisy, kumm." This time Lavina took Daisy's hand, and all but dragged her out of the tree lot.

From where Eli stood, he could hear Daisy complaining all the way. A soft chuckle escaped him at the little girl's determination. It was clear her sister's honesty horrified Lavina, but Eli appreciated honesty.

He didn't have long to think about the sisters before an Englischer called him over to get the price on a tree. A few moments later, Eli was loading a tree onto the back of a truck. When he returned to the tree lot, he had three more customers waiting to be helped.

The rest of the morning flew by in a rush of customers. Eli was grateful for the amount of business, even if it meant he would cut down trees again next week to keep the tree lot stocked.

Now and then he thought of Daisy and her honest admissions. He couldn't help but sympathize with their fate, especially this time of year. It was hard losing a loved one, but it was even harder to face financial difficulties while you were still dealing with grief.

Chapter 4
Poverty Isn't a Sin

As soon as Lavina stepped into the kitchen, she turned to Johanna and Elizabeth. "Would you mind starting with splitting the wood? Take Bonny with you, she can stack them. I need to have a word with Daisy."

Daisy shrank beneath Lavina's gaze. "Please, can they stay?"

Lavina let out an impatient sigh. "Fine they can stay, but we're going to talk about what just happened in town."

Daisy nodded, her eyes wide with anticipation. She clearly knew she had gone a little too far with sharing their personal problems.

"What just happened in town?" Johanna asked curiously.

"Daisy decided it was a good idea to explain to a perfect stranger our entire situation. Starting with Mamm's death, the medical bills we need to pay, and how tight things are at the moment. She even told him about choosing between ground beef and cheese." Lavina shot an angry look at Daisy before she continued. "Then she went on to tell this perfect stranger exactly where we live."

Johanna's eyes widened with horror even as Elizabeth burst out with laughter.

"It's not funny," Lavina insisted.

"It is just a little funny. I can imagine the poor man was just trying to sell a tree and the next moment Daisy is pummeling him with every detail about our lives." Elizabeth continued to laugh. "The poor man is going to think twice before he sells another tree."

Lavina let out a heavy sigh before she turned to Daisy. "Elizabeth might think it's funny, Daisy, but it's not. Some things just aren't meant to be talked about. No one needs to know that we're having a rough time of it. That's our business. Just like they don't need to know that we need to choose between ground beef and cheese."

"I was just trying to explain why we couldn't buy a tree," Daisy said in a small voice.

"And I understand that, but we don't need to explain ourselves to anyone. We simply could've said we weren't interest and walked away." Lavina let out a sigh and shook her head. "I know you don't think that you did anything wrong, but it isn't safe to tell strangers where you live. Mamm taught you that."

"His name is Eli, he told us that himself. So if we know his name, he's no longer a stranger, right?" Daisy asked, crossing her arms.

Lavina couldn't help but shake her head.

"What Lavina is trying to say flower girl, is that there are bad people out there. So we don't tell people we don't know—and knowing their name doesn't mean we know them—where we live. It was wrong of you to run off, and it was wrong of you to tell that man our business, understand?" Johanna took over and cocked a brow with a firm look when she finished.

Daisy's eyes welled up with tears. "I didn't mean to be naughty."

"I know honey, but you need to listen when I tell you stop." Lavina reminded her kindly before she wrapped her in a hug.

"Alright, Lavina, I won't do it again," Daisy promised as she sniffed against Lavina's shoulder. Lavina held her for a few moments longer. Daisy was the youngest and had taken their mother's passing the hardest. Whereas Lavina, Johanna, and Elizabeth were all but grown and didn't need their mother as much anymore, Daisy still need a firm hand and loving discipline.

By the time Daisy's sniffs had stopped, Lavina stood back and searched her gaze. "What do you say we go split some wood?"

Daisy nodded. "Can I help Bonny stack them on the porch?"

"Of course you can," Lavina agreed with a smile.

Daisy and Bonny rushed outside, eager to help, while Lavina, Elizabeth, and Johanna remained behind in the kitchen, not as eager to split wood.

"Was it an Englischer?" Johanna asked curiously.

"Nee, he was Amish. From a different community." Lavina pulled on her work gloves and shook her head. "He was actually very kind; he wasn't impatient with Daisy's babbling at all. I just wish she hadn't said as much."

"Perhaps next time, you and Johanna should go into town and I'll stay here with the younger ones. Before Daisy goes to tell him more personal things about us, like how we struggle to split the wood," Elizabeth suggested.

"That's a gut idea," Lavina agreed. "The more we do it, the easier it will become. I promise."

They headed outside to meet the younger ones beside the house. Lavina couldn't help but sigh at the sight of the five cords of wood that stood beside the house.

The community had been cutting down wood for them each summer, but ever since Johanna, Lavina, and Elizabeth had grown older, no one came to help split the wood anymore. Instead, this chore now fell to them.

Last winter, Lavina had considered asking one neighbor for help, but she felt too bad to ask. Everyone had their own wood to split and Lavina couldn't expect others to do theirs as well. Instead, they had split wood every day, just enough to last them through the night.

That plan had failed miserably.

By the time the heavy snow came, half of their wood had been buried, and they had to chop wood exposed in the harsh winter weather. This year, Lavina had vowed that they would split the wood before the heavy snows fell. That way they could stack it on the porch and no one had to go digging through the snow for wood and try to split it in the middle of a snowstorm.

But it wasn't peaceful work.

Lavina and Johanna each had their own chopping block and axe. While they did the hard work of splitting the wood, Elizabeth would bring the large logs closer for them to have within easy reach. They tasked the younger girls with stacking the wood on the porch.

They worked tirelessly for the next few hours. Lavina excused the little ones to warm up inside while they continued. By the time the sun hung low over the hills, Lavina's arms were burning, her back aching, and her hair a terrible mess.

She turned to look at the logs that had been delivered early in November and let out a heavy sigh. Together, she and Johanna hadn't even split one cord of wood.

"That's it, I can't lift this axe one more time," Johanna complained, dropping the axe into her chopping block. "I have no feeling left in my toes and my arms have turned into rubber."

"Mine too," Lavina sighed. "We'll continue another day. Hopefully, what we split today will last for a couple of days at least."

"Let's hope so." Johanna pulled off her gloves and rolled her shoulders. "If I had money, I would pay someone to do this. I'm sure there is an eager young boy that wants to earn some pocket money somewhere in the community."

Lavina nodded. "If only we had the money."

They headed inside to start on dinner, although both were exhausted. Inside, Daisy and Bonny were playing a board game by the fireplace, blissfully unaware of how hard Johanna and Lavina had worked.

Lavina wouldn't blame them, they were young. They needed to have fun and play, not worry about if there was going to be food on the table by next week and if there was going to be wood to heat the house.

That was her responsibility now.

Chapter 5
The Gift of Christmas

Eli looked at the tree lot and felt a smile curve his mouth. It had been one of the best days he'd ever had selling trees. He had started this morning with almost thirty freshly cut Douglas firs, and only had eight left.

His eye caught the large tree the little girl from that morning had admired and he thought of her sister again. She was now the head of the family by the way she had chastened the little girl. He couldn't imagine how hard it must be for her to care for her sisters whilst dealing with financial insecurity.

Something about the little girl had charmed him, more than he had realized. Her innocence was adorable and her excitement about Christmas was catching. A frown creased Eli's brow realizing that regardless of how much the little girl liked Christmas, she wouldn't have a tree this year.

He looked at the large tree she had admired and felt a smile curve his mouth. He wasn't one to give away trees, besides; it was his family's income, but surely one tree wouldn't make such a big difference?

Eli pulled out his wallet and counted the money he had made during the day. It was much more than he'd expected. His parents would be pleased. He thought of Daisy and

Lavina again and knew that his parents would understand, in fact, they would agree with him that a kind deed was a deed that brought you blessings.

Without hesitation he wrapped up the large tree. He closed up the tree lot for the day, making a mental note of how many trees he would need to bring on Monday, before he loaded the large tree onto his buggy.

On the days he worked at the tree lot, the owner of the hardware store was kind enough to let his horse roam the large yard behind it. Once his horse was hitched to the buggy, Eli headed to the other side of town.

As he drove, he thought of Lavina. Although she had smiled at him kindly, he had seen the shadows in her eyes. Shadows of grief and shadows of guilt of not being able to give her little sister the tree she so badly wanted.

Eli felt anticipation build inside when he turned left at the big tree like Daisy had directed him. He knew that the tree would be met with great excitement by the little girl, but he truly hoped Lavina didn't feel offended by the gift. If he was honest, he was excited to see her again.

Although he was twenty-six years old, Eli had yet to find the right girl to court. He'd attended singings for the first few years after his baptism, he'd even taken a few girls on buggy rides. But not once had he looked at a girl and felt as if he wanted to spend more time with her.

As if he wanted to get to know her better.

When he'd met Lavina that morning, something about her made him want to help lift the shadows from her gaze. He wanted to make her smile without hesitation. He wanted to lift the burden from her shoulders.

He knew he couldn't do all that, but hopefully a Christmas tree might bring a little joy to their Christmas this year.

He spotted the blue house in the distance and felt excitement rush through his veins. The sun was hanging low in the sky, which meant he would probably have to drive home in the dark, but Eli didn't mind.

Without a doubt he knew he was doing the right thing. Christmas was a time for giving, a time for joy, and a time for caring for your neighbor. Lavina and Daisy might not be his neighbors, but something in his heart made him want to help.

He turned right into their yard and noticed the four cords of wood standing against the side of the house. At least he didn't have to worry if they'd be kept warm this winter, he thought, as he stopped the buggy in front of a small barn.

There was a chicken coop to one side of the house and the remnants of a kitchen garden from summer on the other side. The yard was extremely neat, as if every single item had a place. He glanced towards the house and saw smoke bubbling from the chimney. His heart lifted when he saw Lavina through the kitchen window.

When she suddenly turned and looked right at him, he lifted his hand and waved with a smile in place. Perhaps she would surprise him and be grateful for the tree.

Doubt circled his thoughts for the first time, what if she turned him and his tree away?

Pushing the thoughts aside, Eli, climbed off the buggy and waited for Lavina as she watched him with a curious gaze through the kitchen window.

Chapter 6
A Stranger Comes Calling

"That is why you don't go telling strangers where you live," Lavina hissed under her breath at the sight of the man from the tree lot waving to her from his buggy.

"What?" Johanna asked rushing to her side. "Is that him?"

"Jah," Lavina sighed shaking her head. "What has Daisy done?"

"He's quite handsome, Lavina," Johanna said nudging her sister.

"Johanna, hush!" Lavina chastened her.

"Well, are you going to stand here looking at him, or are you going to find out why he came all this way?" Johanna asked with an arched brow.

"Maybe if I pretend like I didn't see him, he'll leave," Lavina mused quietly.

"He's waving, he knows you saw him. Go on, I'll make sure Daisy stays inside," Johanna teased. "Before she tells him we can't split wood or afford new chicken wire for the chicken coop."

Lavina couldn't help but chuckle before she pulled on her coat. "I'll be back soon; I'm just going to ask him to leave."

"You do that," Johanna said with a doubtful look before she turned and headed towards the living room where the other sisters were gathered.

Lavina stepped outside and met Eli's gaze. For a moment she couldn't help but agree with Johanna—he was quite handsome. Not only was he was handsome, he also had a charming smile and kind eyes. She quickly pushed the thoughts from her mind. Now wasn't the time to admire a handsome stranger, it was time to get rid of him.

"Hullo," Eli said as she approached him. "Daisy's directions were quite accurate. Found the place with no trouble at all."

"Hullo," Lavina said cautiously. "And why is that? I mean finding our house? Why did you kumm?"

Eli gestured towards the Douglas Fir that was tied to the buggy. "I brought you a gift. I had a really gut day at the tree lot and although I sold most of my trees, no one seemed to notice how majestic this one was. I knew it was because it actually already had a home."

"We can't afford a tree, Mr. Smucker. I thought my schweschder made that quite clear?" Lavina asked with a cocked brow.

"I didn't ask you to pay me, I said it was a gift."

Lavina frowned. She didn't like charity and she wasn't sure if she wanted a gift from a man they didn't know. "We don't need your charity, Mr. Smucker. Daisy will be fine if she doesn't have a tree this Christmas. I know how much that costs, and you'll be better off selling it in your lot."

"Nee, it's Eli," he said firmly before a smile split his face in two. "And who said anything about charity? I just brought this tree over, because this is where it belongs. So you have one of two choices. Either we stand here arguing in the cold until you finally give in, because I don't give up easily. Or you can help me untie it and carry it inside."

"I'm not taking the tree," Lavina snapped firmly.

Eli took a step towards her and searched her gaze. "Just accept it for what it is, a gift. A gift for Daisy. Surely you can't turn away a gift that isn't even yours?"

Lavina hated he was right. Gott had blessed them in many ways ever since they had lost their mother and now he was blessing them again. Who was she to decide which blessings to accept and which to turn away? "Fine, but for Daisy."

"For Daisy," Eli agreed.

Before Lavina could change her mind, Eli hopped onto the buggy and untied the ropes. Knowing that he wouldn't be able to carry such a large tree inside on his own, she had no choice but to help.

Once they had the tree down from the buggy, Lavina took the front and Eli took the heavier back end. They carried it around the house, towards the porch. Lavina stopped in front of the door for a moment to catch her breath, before she turned to Eli with a warning look. "You realize there are going to be squeals of delight and declarations of your kindness?"

Eli shrugged. "I can handle it."

Lavina opened the front door and as one Bonny, Daisy, and Elizabeth turned to look at them. Daisy's eyes widened with excitement. "A tree! Lavina, you said we couldn't afford one!"

"We can't," Lavina said as she carried the tree into the house. "Eli brought it as a gift, for you."

"For me!" Daisy squealed with delight. "It's the most beautiful tree I've ever seen and now it's going to be right here in our living room."

"I'll get the base," Elizabeth said, moving to a chest where she took out the tree stand.

It took some maneuvering for Lavina and Eli to line up the base of the tree with the tree stand, before Eli slotted it in. Elizabeth quickly adjusted the base to fit snugly around the tree's base, before Eli positioned the tree.

The Douglas Fir stood proudly beside their fireplace. Needles covered the floor but Lavina couldn't even be bothered.

Daisy was right, Christmas wasn't Christmas without a real Christmas tree. She turned to Eli with a look of gratitude. "Denke."

Eli shrugged. "It's a pleasure, besides, this is where it belongs. It's as if it's grown for years just to fit that spot perfectly. The top is just two inches from the ceiling–a perfect fit."

"It's beautiful, Eli. Denke." Daisy rushed towards Eli and threw her arms around his waist in a hug. "It's the best gift ever."

"Now you can smell it anytime you want." Eli smiled down at Daisy making Lavina's heart clench in her chest.

He didn't have to be kind to them and he surely didn't need to drive all the way out here to bless them with the gift of a tree, but he had done it, regardless.

She looked at Eli in a way she had never looked at a man before. His kindness had touched her heart. He turned and smiled at her, and her heart skipped a beat.

She wasn't sure what it was about Eli Smucker, but suddenly Lavina wished she had taken time to fix her appearance after they had split the wood. It probably covered her in dirt, her hair tangled from the wind.

But Eli didn't seem to mind, he met her gaze with a smile, one that warmed her heart.

Chapter 7
A Delightful Dinner

Eli hadn't known how rewarding it would feel to give someone the gift of Christmas. If Daisy's smile wasn't rewarding enough, it was the look of gratitude that Lavina gave him as she mouthed the words thank you.

His heart swelled in his chest, wishing he could do more for the group of women.

He glanced around the house and was surprised with how neat it was. There wasn't a speck of dust in sight. The scent of stew drifted to him from the kitchen, even as he felt his body warm with the heat coming from the fireplace.

Not wanting to intrude more than he already had, he turned to Lavina. "I better be on my way, Merry Christmas."

Lavina was about to answer, when a younger version of her stepped forward. This sister was a few years younger than Lavina but had the same features although her hair was darker. "Nee, please stay. Dinner is almost ready and it would by our way of thanking you for your generosity."

"Eli, this is Elizabeth, she's the middle schweschder," Lavina explained. "That's Johanna, second eldest, and this is Bonny, second youngest."

"Hullo Elizabeth, Bonny, and Johanna. It's nice to meet you all. Denke for the invitation Elizabeth, but I think I've already intruded enough," Eli explained.

"You haven't intruded at all. We're grateful for the company, besides, don't you want to see how pretty the tree looks once Bonny and Daisy decorate it?" Johanna asked with a hopeful smile.

Eli was tempted but glanced at Lavina to make sure she didn't mind.

"You're welcome to stay. As Elizabeth said, it's the least we can do for your generosity. It isn't much, it's just stew," Lavina said with a kind smile.

"You have me convinced," Eli shrugged. "Can I help decorate the tree?"

Daisy nodded eagerly. "We'll fetch the trimmings."

A short while later, Eli took orders from the youngest sisters. Each had their own vision for the tree and it became apparent that Eli's method of just hanging the decorations didn't fit into their plans.

"Nee, Eli. We always hang the paper angels in the middle, see," Daisy instructed. All the decorations were homemade, the brightly painted acorns bringing even more life to the Douglas fir. By the time they were done Eli stood back and slowly clapped his hands.

Daisy and Bonny's vision actually made sense. They had all the earthy items like acorns, starched maple leaves, and twine at the bottom. In the middle there were the paper angels and above them followed the stars. Right at the top of the tree came the large star that had been made with twigs and twine.

"It looks beautiful," Eli admired the tree, wondering why he hadn't thought of decorating his tree in levels before.

"Ach, now it really feels like it's the festive season, doesn't it?" Johanna asked, joining them in the living room.

"It does, Johanna!" Daisy bounced up and down.

"Daisy, Bonny, kumm set the table," Lavina called from the kitchen.

The young girls hurried to the kitchen to do as they were told. Eli turned to Johanna with a curious look. "It must have been hard to lose your mamm, especially with the younger girls."

Johanna nodded. "Very hard. But it's been the hardest on Lavina. She's been a pillar of strength regardless of everything she's had to take on."

"I'm sure you help her?" Eli knew he was prying but he couldn't seem to stop himself.

"Jah, we do. But she takes all the responsibility on her shoulders. It's a heavy weight to carry sometimes. Especially when the little ones act out a little." Johanna chuckled. "But Lavina is great with them, she's firm but kind."

Eli nodded. The more he learned about Lavina, the more he admired the capable woman that she was. He had always respected the fairer sex, especially because he had been raised by a mother who was capable and didn't stand back for anything. But his mother had never faced financial difficulties while raising her younger sisters.

"Dinner is on the table."

Lavina's voice carried to them in the living room. Eli followed Johanna and joined the other sisters in the kitchen.

Eli looked around the table, unsure where he should sit. He knew at their own table everyone had a specific seat they sat in every evening.

"Will you sit next to me?" Daisy asked, looking up at him with a hopeful smile.

"Jah, of course," Eli agreed.

Daisy showed him where to sit and Eli took a seat. Across from them Bonny and Elizabeth had their seats and Lavina and Johanna sat at the heads of the table. Lavina, right beside him.

She smiled at him shyly before she bowed her head. "Let's pray."

In Eli's home they said a silent prayer before dinner, but he quickly learned that things worked a little differently here.

"It's Daisy's turn, I said grace last night," Bonny quickly piped up.

Daisy nodded and once everyone's heads were bowed, she prayed. Not a quick prayer of thanks for the meal but a lengthy prayer revealing even more about their family. Eli couldn't help but smile as he listened.

"And denke for Blueberry for taking us to town. Denke for the purchases we could afford. Please help us afford more on the list next time, Gott. Denke for the Christmas tree, and that Johanna and Lavina could split the wood. Help them do it better, Gott, so that we don't have to do it once the snow sticks to the ground. Denke for the food and denke for taking gut care of Mamm and Daed in heaven. Amen."

By the time Daisy was finished and Eli looked up, he saw another blush of embarrassment cover Lavina's cheeks.

Chapter 8
Honest Confessions

"I give up," Lavina muttered under her breath to Elizabeth beside her before she turned to Daisy with a warm smile. "Denke Daisy, I think you covered everything."

"I tried my best," Daisy said firmly before she took a bite of her stew.

"Just so you know, flower girl," Johanna turned to Daisy with a teasing look, "Lavina and I are doing just fine at splitting the wood."

Daisy frowned. "Then why does it take you so long?"

Lavina chuckled softly beside Eli, it was clear she had absolutely no control over Daisy's words. Daisy still had to learn about thinking before she spoke, but for tonight, Lavina done was chastening her for her honest revelations. "It takes us long because we're not as strong as men."

"Oooh," Daisy said, dragging out the vowels.

As everyone began to focus on their plates, Lavina found herself sneaking a glance at Eli every now and then. It felt strange to have a man at the dinner table. Ever since their father had passed away, it was usually just a group of women around the table.

She remembered a time when her father had still been alive and how much she had enjoyed family dinners back then. Her father would talk about the farm and all his plans, while her mother would praise each of them for the chores they did that day.

Times had really changed, Lavina realized. Their fields haven't been farmed in years and as for their chores, they barely had time to get everything done, never mind praising everyone for their trouble. Chores were part of their lifestyle and unless the chores were done they wouldn't have a Blueberry to take them into town or eggs to harvest from the chicken coop.

Her mother had often reminded her over the last couple of years that it was time Lavina began attending Sunday singings. Every time her mother did, Lavina refused. It wasn't that she didn't want to court or find a husband, but merely because she knew her mother needed her help at home. It was more important for Lavina to quilt and provide an income that would support her family, than it was to go on buggy rides and selfishly dream of her own future.

She snuck another glance and Eli and wondered if she shouldn't have listened to her mother, after all. At least if she had, she would've had a husband to help her support her sisters now. She would've had a husband to help her carry the heavy burden and to be shoulder for her to cry on.

As it was, Lavina made sure that her sisters never knew how hard it was for her, or how much she worried.

Just then, Eli turned and smiled at her, as if he had sensed her watching him. Her heart skipped a beat at his handsome smile.

"Since we can't afford new chicken wire, we can always take the old wire that's still usable from the old coop and use that to fix up the chicken coop." Elizabeth's conversation with Bonny distracted Lavina from the unexpected feeling.

"That can work," Bonny agreed. "I'm not very good with the pliers, but I'm sure we'll figure out. If we don't that fox is going to get in sooner rather than later."

"Jah, he's been sneaking around the chicken coop every night over the last week," Johanna put in.

"The weather looks to hold for a few more days, so we need to try and get as much done as possible before the first snow falls," Johanna pointed out. "Monday morning first thing, Lavina and I are going to start splitting the rest of the wood. Elizabeth, will you get the younger ones to help you with the laundry?"

"Jah, but just remember we still need to fix the barn roof. That cold air might be just a nuisance now, but if the snow falls, it's going to be a right mess," Elizabeth pointed out.

"Jah, you're right. The laundry can wait," Johanna agreed.

"Schweschders," Lavina began feeling a little impatient. "We have a guest, surely we can wait to discuss this another time."

Johanna's eyes widened with surprise. "Ach, I'm sorry Eli. We won't bore you further with everything we need to do."

Eli shook his head and turned to Lavina with a curious look before he turned back to Johanna. "I really don't mind at all. I'm free on Tuesday, I could come by and help. I've been known to have a way with a pair of pliers, and," he turned to Daisy and winked, "I'm strong enough to split logs."

"Nee, we could never expect that of you," Lavina quickly argued.

"You're not expecting it," Eli shrugged. "I'm offering to help. It won't be long before the first snow sticks to the ground and like your schweschder said, these are things that need to be done."

"We'll get them done," Lavina quickly promised. "We've always managed to get things done on time."

"Why struggle on your own, if you have a hand willing to help?" Eli asked her with a searching look.

Lavina felt all her sisters waiting for her answer. If she denied Eli's help, she already knew they would blame her for it later. "We can't pay you, Eli," Lavina admitted quietly.

"I'm not asking for payment. I'll be here Tuesday morning after breakfast," Eli said firmly, making it clear he wasn't going to debate this further.

"Denke, but really, if your plans change or if anything happens, please don't feel obliged to come."

"This stew is really quite gut, your own recipe?" Eli asked, changing the subject.

Lavina wasn't sure if she was irritated or charmed by his insistence to help them. She had turned down offers of help ever since her mother had passed, knowing that she and her sisters needed to learn to get by on their own.

But it seemed it didn't matter how hard she tried, Eli simply wasn't taking no for an answer.

Perhaps instead of fighting against his generosity, she should embrace it and pray for Gott to bless him. She summoned a smile and turned to him. "It was my mamm's recipe. Our favorite."

"It's my favorite too, it's delicious."

Something as simple as complimenting her cooking made Lavina feel powerful. As if although she might be failing her sisters on so many different levels, at least she was doing something right. "Denke."

Chapter 9
Chicken Coop Catastrophe

When Eli explained his plans to his parents on Tuesday morning, they seemed more than a little surprised. Of course, they were proud of him trying to help, but for someone that didn't even bother going to community social gatherings, they were confused why he was so eager to help the sisters he had told them about.

Eli didn't tell them it was because something about Daisy made him want to make life easier for her. Or that something about Lavina made him want to chase the shadows from her eyes. Ever since he had joined them for dinner on Saturday night, Eli hadn't stopped thinking about Lavina.

The more he thought about her, the more he admired her. He prayed for every night, asking Gott to give her strength and the wisdom that she would need to lead her sisters through this difficult time.

He left shortly after breakfast with a small kit of tools that he might need. He wasn't sure what the girls had at their disposal, so he packed his own tools just in case. Tuesdays were the only day of the week that he didn't open the tree lot. Usually, he would spend the time to catch up on chores around the house, but with his father not working in the fields now, all the chores were up to date.

Eli arrived at the blue house a little after nine o'clock. A quick glance at the wood stumps beside the house revealed that Johanna and Lavina had split wood yesterday, but they had barely made a dent in the pile.

First, he would tend to the chicken coop, he decided, then he would focus on splitting the wood. He climbed out of the buggy just as Daisy ran towards him. "Eli, you came!"

"Of course, I came," Eli greeted her with a smile. "I'm a man of my word."

"Everyone's busy with the chicken coop. They started yesterday, but they've made it worse," Daisy said with a frown. "We spent the whole afternoon catching chickens, they all escaped."

Eli nodded as he began to walk around the house to where the chicken coop was located.

"You have to make sure the two pieces of wire are married together, otherwise they'll just escape again," Elizabeth said impatiently as Johanna tried to work with the pliers.

"I'm trying to!" Johanna snapped. "I'm struggling to twist the wire, and it's too short." She pointed to the bottom of the chicken coop where a gap of two inches offered another entrance and exit for a clever chickens.

"Stop fighting, just... give me a minute to think," Lavina said with her back to him.

"Guten mayrie," Eli greeted them with a curious smile. "Having a little trouble there?"

"Eli?" Lavina turned to him with a surprised expression. "You came?"

"I said I would," Eli replied. Why was everyone surprised to see him when he'd said he'd come? "What happened to the chicken coop?"

Johanna glared at Elizabeth before she answered. "Elizabeth thought it would be a great idea to remove a section of the wire before putting up the wire from the old chicken coop. Now we can't find the wire from the old chicken coop and this section seems too small now."

Eli nodded spotting the problem. "Here, let me."

"We need new wire," Johanna said, shaking her head.

"Do you have any wood, maybe a sheet of timber or something?" Eli asked as he began to quickly marry back the two pieces of chicken wire.

"Jah, I think we have some in the barn," Elizabeth replied heavily.

"Right, so for now, I'm going to join these two pieces up. Fetch the sheet then we'll put it on the inside. It will give the chickens a little more shelter from the elements and it will act as a frame to stop this wire from tugging loose," Eli explained.

Three very confused expressions met him, making Eli chuckle. "You girls go do something else, I've got this."

Eli enjoyed fixing things. He especially enjoyed fixing things and improvising ways to make them better. With the chicken coop, he found himself doing just that. Once he had married the two sections of wire back together, he moved around the entire coop, checking it for places that a fox could get through. He inserted the sheet of wood and tied it to the fence, making sure it would act as both frame and shelter.

When he was finally happy with his progress and the result, he began scouring the yard for rocks. Just like they had done at home with their own chicken coop, Eli packed the entire chicken coop with rocks round the bottom. A fox might be able to maneuver his way underneath a chicken wire, but he couldn't move rocks.

"Eli, Lavina says you should come and eat lunch. We've all finished eating already," Daisy announced as she inspected his work. "This is nice."

"Denke. I know, Bonny called me, but I wanted to finish this first."

"And is it finished now?" Daisy asked as if she were the foreman and he a laborer.

"Jah, it's finished. The chickens won't be bothered by the weather, foxes, or any other critter that might want to snatch their eggs." Eli explained patiently.

Daisy nodded, clearly impressed. "Lunch is waiting, I need to go and water the barn animals." She skipped towards the barn making Eli smile.

He stepped into the kitchen, realizing everyone had already moved on with their own chores, except for Lavina who was doing the dishes. With the light catching her hair through the window, she reminded Eli of angel.

"You're here. It's not much, I made peanut butter sandwiches and there's hot kaffe if you want some," Lavina explained, drying her hands on a dish cloth.

"Denke, kaffe will be nice," Eli took a seat at the table and began to eat his sandwich. He couldn't help but feel guilty as he ate. They already had so little and yet they were willing to share. Next time he would bring his own lunch, he promised himself.

Chapter 10
The Negotiations Begin

"Denke so much for your help today, Eli. I don't think you know how grateful we are, especially me. When you arrived this morning Johanna and Elizabeth were almost at each other's throats," Lavina laughed softly. "They're both stubborn and take so much after my daed it's almost unbelievable."

"Was your daed stubborn?" Eli found himself asking.

"Very much so, but in a gut way. When he set his mind on doing something, he'd keep at it until he managed. I remember him building the porch steps repeatedly until they didn't sag. He didn't give up and he didn't ask for help, but he rebuilt them probably four times." Lavina laughed shaking her head.

"Well, the chicken coop has been fixed. No need to rebuild," Eli assured her.

"You're probably eager to get home. You've been here all morning," Lavina pointed out.

"Nee. I still want to split some wood for you, seeing as you and Johanna aren't strong enough," Eli teased.

When Lavina rewarded him with a sweet laugh, his heart skipped a beat. "We'll really manage, you don't have to stay and do it."

Eli held her gaze for a moment. "I want to."

Lavina felt her heart skip a beat. She didn't know if it was Eli's generosity or the kindness in his eyes or simply the way he smiled at her, but something about him affected her heart in a way she didn't understand.

His answer was so simple and yet if she was honest, Lavina would've admitted she wanted him to stay for a little while longer. But she couldn't allow herself that honesty, not now when her sisters needed her the most.

"Alright, but just a few pieces, we'll really manage," Lavina hedged.

Eli's laughter flowed over her; she could almost draw energy from it. "You do realize that it isn't a weakness to accept help. It's a strength to admit when you need it."

Lavina nodded but she didn't respond.

Before she and Eli could continue their conversation, Elizabeth joined them in the kitchen.

"Eli, you've done a wunderbar job with the chicken coop. Denke so much. Do you think you could help me with the barn roof?"

Lavina was about to tell her sister to stop asking him for favors when Eli shook his head. "I'm sorry Elizabeth, not today. I still need to split some wood. I see the pile on the porch has shrunken significantly since Saturday with the cold weather."

"Ach, jah. The wood," Elizabeth sighed heavily. "I guess it's more important for you to help with that, then."

"But I can come by on Saturday afternoon and help you with the roof. I'll ask my daed to run the tree lot in the afternoon, then I can come by?" Eli offered.

"Eli that isn't…" Lavina began but Elizabeth cut her off.

"That's perfect. Denke Eli." Elizabeth turned to Lavina. "You and I both know if I fix it, it won't last."

"Elizabeth," Lavina began to shake her head.

"I've got to go and help Daisy, before she breaks an arm," Elizabeth said glancing out the window.

Lavina followed Elizabeth's gaze only to see Daisy hanging upside down from the washing line. She held her breath as she watched Elizabeth rush towards her and help her down before having a stern word with her.

Disaster averted; she turned back to Eli. "You don't have to, we can manage."

Eli laughed. He stood up and walked towards her. "Since you won't take my help freely, we can negotiate."

"Negotiate how?" Lavina asked feeling her heartbeat just a little faster as Eli stood only a few feet from her.

"I'm coming over on Saturday afternoon. I've already promised Elizabeth. So, either I come and help her fix the barn roof, or I take you on a buggy ride?"

Lavina gasped. "A buggy ride?"

"Jah," Eli nodded. "You know, when two people of certain age go on a buggy ride and get to know each other a little better? If they enjoy it, they might do it again. If they don't, then at least they won't regret not going in the first place."

"I know what a buggy ride is," Lavina said, feeling a little breathless. "I just haven't ever… I haven't had time for such things."

Eli smiled as he moved towards the door. "It's your choice, Lavina. I'd very much like to fix your roof, but I'd like to take you on a buggy ride as well. But right now, I'm going to go split some wood."

Lavina watched him leave the kitchen, feeling more than a little confused. Going on a buggy ride was the last thing she had time for now, but for some reason a buggy ride with Eli sounded nice.

The roof, she quickly reminded herself, she'd let him fix the roof.

Chapter 11
A Fair Trade

"Pass me the salt please," Eli's mother, Ruth, asked from across the table.

Eli blinked twice, realizing he'd been so lost in thought, he hadn't even touched his food yet. He reached for the salt and handed it over to his mother.

"Something on your mind, Eli?"

Eli turned to his mother and shook his head. "Nee, nee. Just lost in thought that's all."

His mother let out a soft chuckle. "I'm very curious about the thoughts you seem to be lost in?"

"I was just wondering if Daed would be able to take over the tree lot tomorrow afternoon?" Eli asked turning to his father.

Daniel Smucker frowned for a moment. "Of course, I don't mind, but could you perhaps tell me why?"

Eli hesitated for a moment. He debated between telling his parents about the five orphaned sisters, or about how he wanted to help Lavina specifically. Finally, he began right at the very beginning, when Daisy had run up to him at the tree lot the week before. When he was done his mother smiled at him with pride shining in her eyes.

"How wunderbaar of you to want to help them," Ruth smiled at her son with approval.

"I have a feeling it's about more than just helping them," Daniel mused, scratching his beard. "Any schweschder in particular you want to help?"

Courtship was a private matter. One that wasn't to be discussed until an engagement had taken place. But Eli didn't have any secrets from his parents, and he wasn't about to start now. "The eldest, Lavina. She's taken all the responsibility on her shoulders to care for her schweschders. It's a heavy burden to carry to alone."

"So you're helping them out, to lighten her load?" his father asked with a cocked brow.

Eli nodded. "Although she refuses to accept my help. She doesn't want anyone to think of them needing charity or sympathy. She tries to be strong and to do everything herself, but certain tasks…"

"Are a mann's work," his father finished for him.

"After I helped them with the chicken coop last week, I offered to help them with the barn roof tomorrow afternoon. It's leaking and if the snow starts to fall, it will cause their hay to mold. Lavina refused to accept my help…" Eli flinched slightly before he continued. "I told her I'd be coming by tomorrow afternoon. It's up to her if she wants me to fix the barn roof or to take her on a buggy ride instead. It was the only way I knew she would let me help with the barn roof."

His father's laughter filled the air even as his mother's soft chuckles sweetened the sound.

"You must like her very much?" Ruth asked curiously.

"I do," Eli admitted. "She's strong and determined, kind and caring, and the most stubborn woman I've ever met. Why doesn't she just accept help when I offer it?"

"Because she's afraid if someone begins to do all the difficult things for her, she'll come to rely on them. Then when they're gone… she'll need to learn all over again," his mother explained with a wisdom that took years to achieve.

"I'll take care of the tree lot tomorrow afternoon, on one condition," his father said with a narrowed look. "Once you've taken care of fixing the barn roof, you insist on taking her on a buggy ride, either way."

"She won't go, Daed, she's stubborn," Eli argued.

His mother laughed softly. "So was your daed. Sometimes, it just takes the right amount of coaxing to convince someone to do something they thought they didn't want to. Later, she'll thank you for it."

"Are you sure?" Eli asked hesitantly. The last thing he wanted to do was to force Lavina to go on a buggy ride with him and to have her hate him for it later.

"Eli, you're twenty-six years old. You've never bothered with buggy rides much before. The mere fact that you suggested it tells me there is something about this girl that intrigues you. Walk the extra mile, do the extra effort, I assure you, you'll thank me later," his father said with an encouraging smile.

Eli nodded. "If you say so."

"We say so. Besides, she might not admit it, but I assure you she's more than grateful for the help you've given thus far. I can't imagine how hard it must be for her to take care of all her schweschders at such a young age."

"I hope you don't mind about the Christmas tree, Daed. They really couldn't afford it. They're still paying her mamm's medical bills, so things are a little tight now," Eli apologized as he explained.

His father nodded. "I don't mind in the least. You did a gut thing, seeh. I'll keep their familye in my prayers, I'll pray that their hardships are over before long."

"Denke Daed," Eli said gratefully.

His mother winked at him with a smile. "Perhaps you didn't give away the tree at all, perhaps you just traded it for love?"

Eli chuckled at his mother's far-fetched words.

But later that night when Eli was curled up in bed, already thinking about seeing Lavina tomorrow, he couldn't help but wonder if his mother hadn't been right.

Lavina truly was a wonderful girl, but there wasn't any talk of love just yet. Before Eli could even consider thinking about love and courting the eldest Schrock sister, he needed to make sure she knew he wasn't helping them out of sympathy.

He was helping them, because it gave him the opportunity to spend more time with Lavina.

Chapter 12
Blackmail & Buggy Rides

"There you go, now all you have to do is press out the shapes and lay them on the baking sheet," Lavina explained to Bonny and Daisy.

Daisy frowned. "Are we really only making one batch of Christmas cookies?"

Lavina's heart grew heavy. "Unfortunately, that's all we can afford. We need the sugar and flour to last until the new year."

"At least we're making cookies," Bonny added brightly.

"We're done," Elizabeth announced, walking into the kitchen with Eli following behind her.

Lavina was caught off guard by his presence.

He had promised to come by on Saturday afternoon and had stayed true to his promise. Eli had arrived shortly after noon and had immediately headed to the barn with Elizabeth to fix the roof.

Lavina had been afraid he wouldn't come, and the roof wouldn't get fixed at all. That was why she and Elizabeth had spent the whole day yesterday, trying to patch it up as best they could.

"You didn't do a too bad job of patching it up," Eli said, moving towards the sheet of cookie dough. "All I had to do was seal it in place and make sure the new seal would hold."

"Denke Eli," Lavina said gratefully. She had known they needed sealant, but she simply couldn't afford to buy sealant now. To learn that Eli had brought sealant along, made her even more grateful for his help.

"Since we finished so quickly, you and Eli can go on your buggy ride and I'll help the little ones with the baking," Elizabeth flashed her a triumphant smile.

Lavina turned to Eli with a surprised look. "But you fixed the roof. That was the deal?"

Eli shrugged. "You began, so our deal fell away. I'll wait for you outside."

As soon as Eli left the kitchen, Lavina turned to Elizabeth with a narrowed look. "He told you about the deal?"

"He did," Elizabeth laughed. "Very original, I might add."

"It's not original, it's blackmail," Lavina huffed.

Elizabeth's smile softened as she searched Lavina's gaze. "Go on the buggy ride, Lavina. Who knows, maybe you'll even enjoy it."

"I have too much to do, I don't have time for buggy rides," Lavina snapped.

Elizabeth cocked a brow. "He's been so helpful Lavina, and I've seen the way you look at each other. Go on the buggy ride, it's the least you can do."

Lavina wanted to argue, but Elizabeth was right. Eli had done so much to help them and all he was asking in return was a buggy ride. She could go on the buggy ride and tell him afterwards she wasn't interested in courting. Then her cards would be on the table and hopefully he'd stop bugging her about it.

"Fine, but I won't be long," Lavina finally said as she reached for her coat.

When Lavina stepped out onto the porch, Eli was waving to her from the buggy. For a moment her heart skipped a beat. She didn't want to go on this buggy ride, so why was she suddenly excited about spending time with Eli?

It didn't make any sense at all.

She crossed the yard and climbed into the buggy. As soon as she was seated, she turned to him with an arched brow. "Do you usually blackmail your way into getting buggy rides?"

Eli's laughter made butterflies take flight in her stomach. "Nee, usually I don't do buggy rides at all. But I knew you wouldn't agree any other way."

Lavina wasn't sure if she should feel flattered. No one had ever asked her on a buggy ride before. To know that he wanted to go on a buggy ride with her so badly that he'd found a way to fool her into going on one, made her even more curious about him.

"I'm not interested in courtship, just so you know. I have my schweschders to take care of, the last thing I have time for is buggy rides and love letters," Lavina turned to him with a firm look.

Eli shrugged. "Gut, at least I know where I stand. Besides, I'm terrible at writing letters. Let's just see this for what it is, a buggy ride."

Lavina was about to tell that him buggy rides equaled courtship, but she held her silence as he turned onto the dirt road. Instead of heading towards the farm lands where numerous members of her community lived, he turned in the other direction.

Curious as to where he was going, Lavina sat back and watched the scenery pass her by. After another two turns, she turned to him with a questioning look. "Where are we going?"

"Nowhere," Eli shrugged. "The scenery along this road is just beautiful this time of year."

"You know it? I thought you lived on the other side of town?" Lavina asked curiously.

Eli chuckled. "Just because I live on the other side of town doesn't mean I don't ever come in this direction. There's a lovely place to have a picnic in summer, right up here by the creek. In winter, the creek is freezing over, but regardless of the trees losing their leaves, it's a pretty spot."

They drove for a while in silence before Lavina turned to him. "Why are you doing this?"

Eli pulled on the reins and brought the horse to a stop. "Because I enjoy your company, and because you're always rushing after your schweschders, taking care of everything. You deserve a little time without having to think about them at all. A little time just to be the Lavina you were before all this responsibility fell to your shoulders."

Lavina's eyes widened with surprise. She hadn't revealed to anyone how she missed just being herself. She longed for the time before her mother became ill, a time where she had enjoyed her sisters' company and didn't have to be responsible for their every need.

She searched Eli's gaze and realized that although she had fought against going on a buggy ride with him, he was right. She needed a little time just to feel like herself again.

"Denke."

"My pleasure." Eli smiled and lifted the reins again before he called to the horse. "Step up."

The horse began to walk just as Eli began to talk. "Tell me how the chickens managed to escape when your schweschders were fixing the chicken coop?"

Lavina laughed at the memory. "Easy, they didn't board up the chicken coop on the inside before they cut out the section of bad wiring." Laughter bubbled from her throat. "It was quite a sight to behold. Fifteen hens running for their lives as Bonny and Daisy tried to catch them, while Johanna was trying to lure the rooster from the roof with a stick of celery."

Eli laughed, shaking his head. "It actually sounds like it could've been a lot of fun."

"It was, but it was a disaster as well," Lavina sighed.

"I am an only child, so I never got to experience what it was like to have a lot of siblings. I can imagine it can be both fun and exhausting."

"It is," Lavina agreed. "Especially when everyone is so different from each other. Elizabeth is stubborn just like our daed used to be. No one can tell her anything. If she can't find a way to do something, she'll keep trying until she gets it right. Then there's Daisy, she's just kind and sweet and just wants to be happy."

"And you? What are you like Lavina?" Eli asked, glancing at her with a curious look.

Lavina frowned. "I'm not sure. I'm not as stubborn as Elizabeth, or as disciplined as Johanna. I guess in a way I'm a little like all of them. I enjoy doing chores, the satisfaction of knowing something had been done in the right way. I enjoy quilting, have ever since I can remember. And I love cooking. Other than that, it's hard to tell you what I'm like."

"You missed out a few things," Eli said with a smile. "You missed out the part about how you are loving, caring, and firm but gentle. You didn't say that you enjoy gardening, Elizabeth told me," Eli added. "And you left out the part about being a wunderbar caretaker for your schweschders. A person's true character isn't shown in times of wealth and good harvests, it's shown in the face of adversity. I'd say your character is quite admirable."

Lavina felt a light blush color her cheeks. When Eli looked at her like that, she forgot about her sisters and all the responsibilities she had at home. It felt as if he could look right into her soul and see the person she was inside. It was a powerful feeling, one that made her heart swell with emotions she couldn't recognize.

"I'm not sure I'm all that..." Lavina said shyly.

Eli turned to her with a smile. "You're right, you're so much more. Ready to start heading home?"

"Already?" the words escaped Lavina's mouth before she could stop them.

Eli chuckled softly. "We've already been gone for more than an hour and a half."

"What?" Lavina asked, surprised. "Jah, we'd better head home."

As they drove back to the Schrock homestead, Lavina was surprised how much she had enjoyed the buggy ride. So much so that she had completely lost track of time. She glanced at Eli and found herself wondering if it was because it was with Eli, or because she simply had no responsibilities for a short while.

By the time he turned into their yard, Lavina knew the answer.

It was because of Eli.

She wouldn't try and figure out the emotions he awakened within her heart just yet, but for now, she would secretly hope that he would blackmail her into another buggy ride soon.

Chapter 13
A Schweschder's Concern

"Daisy and Bonny are fast asleep," Johanna said as she walked into the kitchen. "And our dear schweschder Elizabeth is lost in a book about gardening. Who reads gardening books in the middle of winter?"

Lavina laughed softly with a shrug. "Our dear schweschder, Elizabeth."

"Kaffe?" Johanna asked, moving towards the wood stove.

"Nee, I've just put on a pot of tea." Lavina took a seat at the kitchen table. "Will you join me for a cup?"

"Jah, tea sounds lovely." Johanna sat down and smiled at the plate of cookies in the center of the table. "It was nice of you to let them bake. I know we couldn't really afford the extra sugar and butter, but it gave them at least a small taste of our usual Christmas traditions."

Lavina nodded. "I couldn't let Christmas come without them having any of our usual traditions at all." A chuckle escaped her. "Although I doubt these cookies are going to last until Christmas."

"Let them eat them," Johanna said with a smile speaking of memories of the past. "Do you remember how we used to stuff our aprons with cookies? We never could tire of them. I swear Mamm baked probably a dozen batches every Christmas."

"A dozen and a half batches," Lavina corrected her. A soft sigh escaped her. "I miss her, especially now, this time of year."

"We all do. You need to realize Lavina, no one is expecting you to take Mamm's place. You don't have to do everything she did. You still have your own life to live as well." Johanna met her gaze with a cocked brow.

"I'm not taking Mamm's place, I'm just trying to make sure we get by without anyone feeling left out or looked over," Lavina defended herself.

"Elizabeth and I can take care of ourselves. Stop worrying about us. It's the little ones we need to look out for, there's three of us, Lavina, and only two of them. You should stop carrying the burden by yourself."

"It's not a burden to care for them or for you," Lavina responded quickly.

"I know, Lavina, I just meant… Elizabeth still goes to visit her friends, I still go to prayer group and I spend time at the farm stall. What do you do for yourself?"

"I quilt," Lavina shrugged.

"You quilt because we need the money. Today was the first time in four months you did something simply because you wanted to. Wasn't it fun to let go of all the worries and responsibilities for a short time?" Johanna asked just as the teapot began to whistle. "I'll make the tea."

Lavina thought about her sister's words for a moment before she finally answered. "I didn't go because I wanted to, I went on the buggy ride because Elizabeth all but bullied me into it."

"You're not answering my question. Did you enjoy it?" Johanna asked firmly this time. She set down a cup of tea in front of Lavina and joined her at the table with a questioning look.

Lavina finally let out a sigh. "I did. It was nice to just talk and not worry about what Daisy was up to or where Bonny was off too. But at the same time, I felt guilty for not being home. I felt guilty for having fun because I'm supposed to grieve Mamm still."

"Says who?" Johanna asked rolling her eyes. "We each grieve in our own ways and to be honest, Mamm was sick for a while. We knew she was slowly fading away. In our own way we began to say goodbye weeks before she passed away. She would've wanted us to be happy, Lavina. She wouldn't have wanted us to sit at home and mourn her forever."

"That's not what I'm doing," Lavina said heavily.

"Nee? Just because you're not crying all the time, doesn't mean you're not putting your life on hold. Ever since Mamm passed away, everything you've done, every decision you made, was for us. It's time for you to think of your own life and your own dreams for the future, Lavina. Eli seems like a gut mann, if you enjoyed spending time with him, do it again. It's as simple as that."

Lavina frowned and shook her head. "I don't think he really likes me; I think he pities me. I don't want his pity or his charity."

"Then don't accept it. But remember, there is nothing wrong with accepting a little help. Especially from a gentleman who is eager to spend time with you."

"Are you done?" Lavina asked impatiently.

Johanna laughed. "Not by a long shot, but that's enough for tonight." Johanna reached for Lavina's hand and searched her gaze. "Ever since I can remember you've helped Mamm take care of us. When Daed passed away you stepped into his shoes although you were still young. I just don't want you to think that your future belongs to us. If you do that, you'll end up all alone when we all move on and start families of our own. Just remember that schweschder."

The picture Johanna painted made for a bleak one. Lavina swallowed past the fear that it brought and smiled at her sister. "Denke, I'll keep that in mind."

"Gut, because you're already twenty-four. It's time to start thinking of a familye of your own and not just ours," Johanna pointed out.

"I thought you were done?" Lavina teased.

"I am done. I just... I worry about you, that's all," Johanna said with a kind look.

"Denke," Lavina smiled at her sister.

They talked about the young girls and finished their tea, but although Lavina pretended that Johanna's words didn't bother her, they bothered her enough to keep her up for most of the night.

Perhaps Johanna was right. Perhaps it was time for Lavina to let Johanna and Elizabeth carry some of the burden, so that she could start thinking about her own future.

Chapter 14
The Lord Repays Graciousness to the Poor

On Saturday evening, Eli arrived home with a skip in his step and a song in his heart. Whatever expectations he'd had for a buggy ride with Lavina, had been exceeded.

For the first time in his life, he found himself eager to see a girl again. He found himself thinking of her all the time. It was an exciting feeling, one that he hoped would not only lead to more buggy rides, but would lead to a future with the oldest Schrock Sister.

Ever since he had driven away from the Schrock homestead this afternoon, an idea had begun to take form in his mind. He wasn't sure how would be able to bring it to life, but he knew that he wanted to try.

Once they had finished dinner, Eli sought out his mother, knowing that she'd been part of community projects in the past. Not only would she be able to point Eli in the right direction, but hopefully she'd be willing to help.

"Mamm, do you have a minute? There is something I'd like to discuss with you?"

Ruth smiled curiously at her son. "You didn't blackmail that poor girl into another buggy ride, did you?"

Eli chuckled. "Nee. Next time I'd like her to come willingly."

"Gut." His mother smiled at him with approval. "What do you want to discuss with me?"

Eli drew in a deep breath and hoped his mother would understand. "I told you how Lavina is struggling to get by with all the medical bills they have to pay?"

"Jah, you mentioned they're having a hard time of it?"

"They're having a tough time, Mamm. Lavina and the two older schweschders understand why things are a little tight now, but the two younger ones, Bonny and Daisy, they don't really understand why they can't have a normal Christmas. Especially after just having lost their mamm."

"Is it really that bad?" Ruth asked with a frown.

Eli nodded. "It is Mamm. They can't afford to even bake cookies this year, a Christmas tradition that has been in their familye forever. I can't imagine they'll even be able to afford a ham for Christmas. I just can't understand why doctors and the hospital can't be a little more lenient when someone has passed away?"

"It's business, it's the Englisch." His mother shrugged with a heavy sigh. "I don't think we'll ever understand their greed."

"That's why I need your help." Eli held his mother's gaze. "I know they're not from our community, but it's become clear to me that Lavina won't ask for help from her own community. She doesn't want to be pitied or accept charity."

"Pride isn't a strength, my seeh…" Ruth trailed off.

"I think it's more for the sake of the younger girls, Mamm. I can only imagine how horrifying it would be for Daisy to return to school only to have the other kinner tease her because they couldn't afford their own food. She's protecting them, Mamm, and it's making it hard for her."

"So, what do you have in mind?"

"I want to see if we can have a small fundraising here, in our own community? The farmers had gut harvests this year, Mamm. I'm sure if we explain Lavina's situation, they will be willing to contribute. If every family can donate just a tin of food or a few ounces of sugar it will make a big difference for the Schrock schweschders." Eli explained, hoping his mother would be willing to help him.

She reached for his hand and smiled at him. "Eli Smucker, you have become a gut mann. Of course, I'll help. When it comes to asking money, people are hesitant, but food donations – of course our community will contribute."

"You really think so Mamm? I was thinking of surprising them with a food hamper on Christmas morning," Eli explained.

"I think it's the best idea ever. You focus on helping your daed with the tree lot and I'll focus on making sure the Schrock schweschders have a wunderbaar food hamper on Christmas morning."

"Denke Mamm." Eli smiled gratefully at his mother. "Like I said, anything would help. At least if they don't have to buy food, they can pay off the debts from the hospital a little faster."

"Gott blesses us to share our blessings."

His mother smiled at him one last time before she left and joined his father in the living room by the fire. Eli retired to his bedroom and couldn't help but feel sympathy for Lavina and her sisters. He was blessed to still have both of his parents present in his life. To have their advice and their support; he couldn't imagine losing them.

That evening when Eli said his prayers, he thanked the Lord for his parents, and he asked the Lord to provide and care for the Schrock sisters. He also asked the Lord to guide the feelings he had for Lavina, and to open her heart to him.

Eli finally fell asleep with hope in his heart, knowing that although he personally couldn't make a difference for Lavina and her sisters, with the help of his mother and the generosity of their community, it was now only a matter of time.

Chapter 15
Arranging Priorities

On Sunday evening, Lavina found herself wandering through the house, aimlessly. Last night, she had struggled to fall asleep after Johanna's firm words about her living her own life. But tonight, she couldn't help but feel a little lost.

Her life was this house. Her life was her sisters. How could she think of a future without them?

Once all her sisters had turned in for the night, Lavina made herself a cup of tea and went to sit out on the porch. Wrapped up in a blanket and armed with a steaming cup of tea, she took a seat on the rocking chair and felt grief wash over her.

How many nights had she sat on this porch with her mother? It had been their time, when the house had already gone to sleep and there was nothing to distract their attention. It had been during those nights that they had discussed their plans. They had talked about the expenses and how much they could afford to save.

Lavina knew that her sisters wouldn't ever understand that when they had lost their mother, Lavina had lost her best friend. Ever since she could remember, Lavina hadn't had a need for the company of girls her own age. Her mother had been her closest friend, her confidante, and her mentor. Caring for her sisters was something Lavina had done for as long as she could remember, but what made it hard now was not having her mother to turn to for advice or support.

What would her mother have done?

The question circled in Lavina's mind as her breath escaped in white puffs into the cold evening air. Her mother had always made certain they had savings to turn to in times of need. But when her mother had become ill, it had been Lavina's decision to use their savings to pay for her mother's treatment.

Little did she know the treatment would be too little too late.

But at least it had given them a few more months with their mother, she consoled herself. If it hadn't been for the treatments, they would've lost their mother much sooner.

Now that they didn't have any savings to turn to, Lavina was at a loss. They didn't have an extra source of income to help them meet the financial demands of the bills now. It was winter, which meant they couldn't even grow their own produce. Altogether it was just a combination of elements that made this the most challenging Christmas Lavina had ever had to face.

But she didn't want her younger sisters to suffer or feel bereft in any way?

She found herself glancing around the yard and couldn't help but notice how much Eli had helped them over the last couple of weeks. A smile curved her mouth as she remembered the buggy ride he had taken her on. Lavina hadn't expected to enjoy it, never mind hope to go on another buggy ride in future, but she did.

A sigh escaped her, wishing there was a way she could scrape together the funds for her mother's medical bills. Even if she couldn't pay them now, just a little more time would give her chance to take a breath.

The empty rocker beside her caught her gaze and Lavina felt that familiar rush of grief. It had been on this porch that her mother had confessed to her about being ill. Everyone had turned in for the night and her mother had invited her to join her for tea. It had been a cold evening in January, the entire yard was white with snow.

She could still remember the fear in her mother's words when she told Lavina that she didn't have a stomach bug. Instead, the doctor had found something much worse: cancer.

A tear slipped over Lavina's cheek at the memory. That night she had sat with her mother for hours, neither of them saying a word, both just trying to understand the challenges that lay ahead.

Lavina hadn't for one moment thought she would lose her mother because of it.

She took the last sip of her tea and retreated into the welcoming warmth of the house. She had barely climbed into bed when she heard the soft tread of someone's footsteps in the hallway. A smile curved her mouth, already knowing the footsteps would be coming towards her bedroom.

Lavina turned up the oil lantern beside her bed and smiled when Daisy appeared in the doorway. Tears covered her cheeks, her hair all mussed and tangled from sleep.

"Did you have a nightmare?" Lavina asked as she patted the space beside her on the bed.

Daisy rushed over and hopped onto the bed. "Jah, another one about Mamm's funeral. Can I sleep with you tonight? I miss her"

Lavina bit back the tears that burned her eyes. She wrapped her arm tightly around Daisy and pressed a kiss to the top of Daisy's head. "Of course you can. I miss her too."

Daisy's breathing deepened a few moments later, and she fell asleep in Lavina's arms, holding on as if she would never let her go.

Lavina smiled, grateful that Daisy had her. She would never be able to take their mother's place, but at least Daisy knew that Lavina would always be there for her.

Lavina's mind turned to Johanna's words of the night before. She glanced down at Daisy and let out a quiet sigh. How could she even consider thinking of her own future, when Daisy and Bonny relied on her?

It was easy to agree to share the burden and to allow Eli to court her, but now as she lay in her bed with Daisy tucked in beside her, Lavina realized the reality was much more complicated. What man would want to court a woman that had two young girls to care for? Even if she relieved herself of the burden of caring for Johanna and Elizabeth, there would still be Bonny and Daisy.

She could no more turn her back on them than she could have turned her back on her mother when she had needed her most.

Lavina felt caught between her present and her future and wasn't sure how she would ever be able to get from the one to the other. She liked Eli; she appreciated his kindness. A short while ago she would've eagerly admitted that she was looking forward to going on another buggy ride with him.

But how could she lead Eli on, knowing that she couldn't give up her responsibility for Bonny and Daisy? No man would want to marry a woman who came with two young girls that weren't her own.

A tear slipped over Lavina's cheek, realizing that courtship simply wasn't possible at the moment.

Johanna might call it a sacrifice, but for Lavina it was a privilege to be able to take care of her younger sisters. A privilege that broke her heart.

She leaned back and closed her eyes, hoping that the Lord would hear her prayers and give her the answers she so desperately needed.

"Dear Gott, denke for all the blessings you have bestowed on our familye. Denke for food in our bellies, for a warm bed and roof over our head. I realize that we complain about not having enough to celebrate Christmas like we always do, Gott, but I also realize there are folks that have even less.

I ask not for myself, Gott, but for Bonny and for Daisy. Help me find a way to give them the Christmas they deserve. Help me find a way to make ends meet, to be the pillar of strength my familye needs now.

Gott, then I want to ask you to bless Eli. The kindness he has shown towards me and my familye, has been such a blessing. Denke for bringing him into our lives, Gott, but please help him understand that courtship simply isn't possible for me.

Please help me forget about these feelings he has awakened in my heart, help me diminish the hope I have for a future with him. My priority is my schweschders, Gott. I simply cannot afford to think of anyone else right now.

I beg of you to guide me on this path, Gott. This path you have chosen for me. I know you won't give me any challenge you do not think I am capable of overcoming. Now I look to you for guidance. Guide my steps, my heart, and my choices.

Bless my schweschders, Gott. Bless our home and bless our familye this Christmas.

Amen."

Chapter 16
An Unwelcome Visit

Eli wasn't sure if the gift would be welcomed or frowned upon, but it gave him an excuse to visit the Schrock homestead again on Wednesday.

Once the tree lot had been closed for the day, Eli found himself driving towards the other side of town. His mother hadn't wasted a single minute with their charity drive for the Schrock sisters. Every night when Eli arrived home, there was more food in the box by the front door.

Just like gossip travelled quickly in their small community, news of someone needing help travelled just as fast.

But that wasn't why Eli was going to visit the Schrock family today.

On Monday he had helped his mother clear out the storage shed beside the house. Most of the items that had been gathered there over the years were nothing more than rubbish. But between the rubbish he found something, he knew would bring a smile to a little grieving girl's face.

The box of wooden tree ornaments had been a gift from his father one Christmas. There had been too many for Eli to hang on the Christmas tree. So instead, Eli had selected his favorites and had painted them to hang on the tree.

Those ornaments still graced their Christmas tree every year, but the box with left over wooden ornaments had been in the shed ever since. Eli had brought the box with ornaments along with some paint for Daisy. Since he knew that they couldn't afford to embrace all their usual Christmas traditions, Eli hoped that painting ornaments for the Christmas tree would at least be small consolation prize.

He pulled into the yard just as the sun sank over the hills in the west.

As he climbed out of the buggy, Bonny and Daisy came rushing towards him. "Eli! Hullo!"

Eli laughed. "Hullo girls."

Lavina followed them with a hesitant smile. "Hullo Eli, this is a surprise."

Eli smiled at her, hoping to see her eyes light up like they had on their buggy ride. Instead, she offered him a cool smile with a question in her gaze.

Eli removed the box from the buggy and held it up. "I brought a gift for Daisy actually."

"You don't have to bring us gifts," Lavina said quickly.

Eli shook his head. "I'm not bringing you gifts; I'm bringing something for Daisy. We were clearing out the storage shed behind the house, and I just knew she'd love it."

"What is it?" Daisy asked eagerly, trying to jump high enough to see into the box. Daisy was completely unaware of the disproving look Lavina was giving Eli.

"It's wooden ornaments for your Christmas tree. My daed made them a long time ago. He made too many, so these have been in the shed for years. I also brought paint, so you and Bonny can paint them any colors you like." Eli set the box down on the ground.

Bonny and Daisy eagerly began to dig through the different shapes.

"Look Lavina, a star!" Bonny held up a star shape.

"Is this a snowflake?" Daisy asked with the shape in her hand.

"Jah, that's a snowflake," Eli confirmed.

"Girls, say denke to Eli, then take the box inside," Lavina said firmly.

Bonny and Daisy said thank you before they carried the box towards the house together. Eli turned and looked at Lavina with a questioning look. "Everything all right?"

"Jah, why wouldn't it be?" Lavina asked cocking a brow.

"You seem... a little off?" Eli shrugged with an apologetic look. "I'm sorry for just showing up, but I thought Daisy might enjoy painting the ornaments."

"Denke," Lavina sighed. "It was very kind of you. You'll have to excuse me, but I have food on the stove."

Eli wasn't sure if he'd offended her or if he'd misread their buggy ride, but the Lavina standing in front of him now, wasn't the same person he'd met in the past. He reached for her hand when she began to turn and searched her gaze. "Lavina, are you angry with me?"

Lavina shook loose from his grip. "Of course not. Why would I be angry with you?"

"Alright, then how about you agree to another buggy ride. I can come on Saturday afternoon?" Eli asked hopefully.

Lavina took a step back and searched his gaze for a moment before she answered. "Although I appreciate the offer, Eli, now simply isn't a gut time for buggy rides."

"I wasn't asking you to go on a buggy ride, now, I was asking if I could take you on one on Saturday afternoon?" Eli frowned, he wasn't sure why she was acting so aloof, but it made his heart sting with pain.

"Now, in general, isn't a gut time. This is our first Christmas without Mamm, I need to be there for my schweschders, not gallivanting on buggy rides with a mann I hardly know."

If she had slapped him, it would've hurt less. Eli took a step back, feeling as if she had just thrown up a wall of ice. "I'm sorry you feel that way."

"I'm glad you understand. Now if you'll excuse me, I need to get back inside. Denke for the ornaments." Lavina attempted a smile, but it seemed forced.

She turned and walked away, leaving Eli standing by his buggy.

For a moment he just stood there feeling as if someone had tugged out the earth from under him. He'd been so certain that he and Lavina had shared a connection, now he couldn't help but wonder if he had imagined it.

Finally, he climbed into the buggy and took the reins. But as he turned the buggy, he caught sight of Lavina watching him from the kitchen window. She lifted her hand in a wave, a sad smile on her face.

It confused Eli even more.

Not knowing what else to do, Eli quietly began to pray, hoping the Lord could make more sense of what had just happened than he could.

"Dear Gott, please help me understand what just happened. A few days ago, I was certain Lavina felt the same way as I do. But now... she seems cold and distant. Did I do something to offend her Gott? Was the gift a blow to her pride? Please Gott, help me..."

As if the Lord had whispered into his ear, the answer came to Eli.

Lavina wasn't refusing to go on a buggy ride because she didn't like him, she felt torn between her responsibility to her sisters and her own future.

When Eli prayed again, he asked the Lord to open Lavina's heart to love and to help her understand that he would never ask her to choose between him and her sisters.

Chapter 17
Selling Dreams

It was exactly one week before Christmas when Lavina opened the pantry and found the sugar container was empty.

Tears burned her eyes. She couldn't help but feel as if she had failed her sisters. Without saying a word, she retreated to her bedroom and opened her hope chest. Since she had been baptized, Lavina had begun collecting items for her own home one day. Right on top lay the wedding quilt her mother had gifted her on her twenty first birthday. Simply the sight of her mother's handiwork, made the tears escape.

Lavina held it to her chest as she allowed herself to grieve for her mother and for everything she couldn't provide for her sisters. She sat like that for a long time until she had gathered enough courage to look further.

Setting the wedding quilt aside, Lavina began to unpack her hope chest. She found the set of cups and matching plates she had bought after selling her very first quilt. There were nightdresses, prayer kapps, and numerous other items she had made for when she was a married woman.

There were also items like oil lanterns, quilts she had made for her own home, including an heirloom quilt she had made for her firstborn. It was the prettiest quilt Lavina had ever made, the only quilt she had vowed never to sell.

But with no sugar in the pantry and no money in her purse, Lavina knew she didn't have any other choice. The wedding ring quilt her mother had made would fetch a better price, but Lavina would rather sell her soul than sell the quilt her mother had made for her.

She carefully packed everything back into her hope chest, keeping the heirloom quilt aside. Knowing that both Johanna and Elizabeth wouldn't let her sell it, she wrapped it in brown paper before she made sure her face didn't reveal her crying.

Armed with the heirloom quilt, she told her sisters she had forgotten about a last delivery before Christmas. She didn't wait for Elizabeth or Johanna to ask the questions they revealed in their surprised looks.

Before they could question her, Lavina took the buggy and left for the farmstall. Barley an hour later she had enough money in her purse for sugar and a few other items, as well as the next installment of the medical bills that would be due in the coming week.

She stopped by the store and returned home just before lunch, only to be met with great excitement. Her heart was shattered for having to sell the heirloom quilt, it had symbolized her dreams of one day having a child, a family of her own. Pushing her heartache aside, she set down her purchases on the kitchen table.

"What's going on?" Lavina asked as she glanced around the kitchen.

"This arrived in the mail," Elizabeth explained handing Lavina the envelope.

Curiously, Lavina opened the envelope and pulled out a beautiful Christmas card. But it was the words inside that made her breath catch.

To the Schrock Schweschders.

You are hereby cordially invited to join the Smucker familye for Christmas lunch at their home. We would love to welcome you at our table and have you share in our feast of ham, sweet peas, baked potatoes, carrots, and baked pumpkin pie. For dessert we have a variety of pies as well as baked pudding planned.

Your presence will warm our hearts this season.

Unless otherwise informed, we will prepare to spend the day with you. You can find the address below this invitation.

Festive Greetings

Eli, Ruth, and Daniel Smucker

"Isn't it wunderbar?" Bonny asked brightly. "You said we couldn't afford a ham, now we don't have to."

"Bonny, we can't just join them for Christmas lunch. We don't even know these people," Lavina argued, feeling a little uneasy. She knew this was Eli's doing and although it was kind and generous of him, she didn't want him to feel as if he had to invite them to Christmas lunch because they couldn't afford to cook one of their own.

"Lavina, living room, please?" Johanna said firmly with a cocked brow.

Lavina sighed impatiently and followed Johanna into the living room. "You know we can't accept that invitation. Eli feels sorry for us. It's not right for us to intrude on their Christmas celebrations."

Johanna crossed her arms and narrowed her eyes. "Are you quite finished?"

Lavina's eyes widened at Johanna's cross tone. "Jah."

"Gut. First, no one asked Eli to invite us. Second, the invitation is from Eli and who I take to be his parents. Third, will you really decline that invitation, knowing that it will be gut for us to go? Not only will Bonny and Daisy be able to have a traditional Christmas feast, but it will mean they won't sit at home on Christmas day missing Mamm and not even having the privilege of a dinner to look forward to? I know you're proud and I know you like Eli, so what is the problem?" Johanna finally finished, slightly out of breath.

Lavina let out a heavy sigh. "It just doesn't feel right. Eli didn't ask Daisy to blabber about our troubles. I just feel as if Daisy had dumped all of this on him, without even realizing it. And as for Eli and I, the buggy ride was a mistake. I have too much on my plate now to even consider courtship."

Johanna chuckled sarcastically. "Eli knows Daisy is just a child. This invitation isn't because of Daisy. And as for you having too much on your plate, you hardly have anything on your plate, remember that. And courtship – you can't make an appointment for love to arrive Lavina, if it comes knocking you either open the door or you don't. Just remember, regret always comes too late."

Not wanting another speech from Johanna about love, Lavina shrugged. "Fine, we can go."

"Gut. Now, where did you get money to go to the store?" Johanna asked, arching a brow.

"I made a plan," Lavina shrugged.

"Lavina, you didn't have any other deliveries to make before Christmas. That means you either sold— You sold the heirloom cot quilt, didn't you?" Johanna shook her head even as she moved towards Lavina and wrapped her in a bear hug. "I'm so sorry schweschder. You didn't tell me because you knew I wouldn't allow it."

"We needed sugar," Lavina said, biting back the emotion welling up inside her.

Johanna pulled away and met Lavina's gaze. "You're not selling anything else from that hope chest, understand? We can skip a payment on the bills rather than have you sell your dreams. Understand?"

Lavina smiled sadly. "I understand."

"Gut, now let's go tell the girls we're going for Christmas lunch at the Smuckers." Johanna wrapped her hand through Lavina's elbow and led her into the kitchen. "We're going!"

Bonny and Daisy squealed with excitement.

"Can I make Eli a gift?" Daisy asked hopefully. "I found an ornament shaped like a flower in the box he brought over. I can paint it like a Daisy. Then if he hangs it on their tree, he'll always remember us?"

"That's a great idea," Johanna encouraged her.

Lavina smiled at Johanna and for the first time she realized Johanna wasn't a little girl anymore. She could confide in Johanna and if she needed to, she could lean on Johanna, like she was doing right now.

Wasn't that what sisters were for?

Chapter 18
Their Mysterious Christmas Angel

Before dawn, Eli met his mother in the kitchen. The woodstove was crackling after just being stoked with more wood and coals as the kettle whistled to announce the tea was ready.

"Gut, you're up," Ruth said as she continued to pack things into the largest basket Eli had ever seen.

Eli rubbed the sleep from his eyes and shook his head. "Mamm, when you said you managed to get a few things together, I never realized it would be this much."

His mother's laughter was soft in the quiet morning hours before the sun rose with a new day. "I told you that our community is generous, especially after the gut harvests they had this past year."

"Do you think they'll accept it?" Eli asked as he poured some tea for him and his mother.

Two days ago, his mother had suggested that he surprise the Schrock sisters on the morning of Christmas Eve instead of on Christmas day. That way they would have two days of being spoiled, instead of just one.

Eli's biggest fear was that Lavina wouldn't accept the basket if she knew it had been orchestrated by him. At first, he had considered delivering it in person, but after discussing his plan with his mother, she had agreed, it would be better to leave it on their porch as a surprise.

"I'm sure they will. It's easier to accept a little charity when you don't have to look someone in the eye. If you leave it on the porch, like you have planned, I'm sure they'll be over the moon when they begin to unpack it," Ruth explained as she began to scribble a note.

"Don't tell them it's from us," Eli quickly warned his mother.

"I'm not telling them anything. I'm simply leaving a bible verse to give them a little hope. It seems to me that a little hope is exactly what these girls need, along with a full pantry," Ruth explained as she tucked the note into the basket.

Eli moved to his mother's side and wrapped an arm around her shoulder. "Denke Mamm. Gott really blessed me to have a mamm like you."

"Ach, what are you talking about. He blessed me to have a seeh like you. A seeh that wants to help and recognized need. You're a gut mann, Eli. I just hope this Lavina-girl realizes it before it's too late."

Eli chuckled. "There's time yet."

"Sure there is. Now you'd better swallow your tea and load this on the buggy. The sun will be rising soon, you don't want to be caught on their porch in the light of day. People might think you're a burglar."

Eli nodded and swallowed down his tea. What his mother didn't know was that secretly he wanted to be a burglar; he wanted to be the burglar that stole Lavina's heart.

***

Although the farmstall wasn't buying anymore quilts until the new year, Lavina had spent the last few days quilting at the speed of light. The more quilts she had to sell when the new year came, the sooner they could find their way out of the deep well of debt.

Her hands had been cramping when she had crawled into bed just before midnight the night before, but Lavina didn't mind. She had never minded hard work.

Light seeped through the curtains of her room as she stretched out in bed. Her hands were still sore from all the quilting, but at least she had managed to finish two single bed quilts this week. For the next few days, she wouldn't be touching her quilting.

Starting with today, it was Christmas time.

It was the morning of Christmas Eve and before Lavina even managed to climb out of bed, she remembered that it would be their first Christmas without their mother. Her heart clenched with grief in her chest as she took a moment to remember her mother. Once she climbed out of bed, she needed to find the energy to be in good spirits for her sisters.

A few moments later, she pushed back the covers and climbed out of bed. She pulled on her robe just as she heard the crunch of footsteps in the snow outside her window.

Curious, since her sisters would still be asleep, Lavina moved towards the window.

She caught sight of a figure walking towards their porch. For a moment fear stole her breath, until she saw the figure placing a large basket at their front door. She couldn't be sure, but it seemed the basket was filled with food and pantry items.

A frown creased her brow just as the figure retreated from the porch and moved towards her window again. Her heart skipped a beat, when he stopped and looked up right at her.

Eli.

Her heart swelled in her chest with affection. She couldn't fathom why he would bring them a basket filled with goods after the way she had treated him. He smiled up at her warmly before he waved and walked off through the snow again.

For a moment, Lavina just stood there. Perhaps she had been wrong about Eli pitying them. Perhaps he really cared. Her heart swelled at the thought, remembering how much she had enjoyed their buggy ride.

If it were a different time and if she hadn't had her sisters to care for, Lavina could admit that she would've enjoyed spending more time with Eli.

Once she had dressed and combed her hair, Lavina headed to the kitchen only to find Elizabeth and Daisy already enjoying a cup of tea. "Merry Christmas!" Lavina greeted them with a bright smile.

Elizabeth frowned. "It's Christmas Eve, not Christmas day."

"Either way, I wish you both a merry Christmas," Lavina repeated pouring herself a cup of tea. She glanced at the two pieces of wood beside the wood stove and carefully pushed them out of sight. "Bonny, would you mind fetching us some wood from the porch?"

Bonny let out a sigh of grievance. "Really, now?"

"Please, denke," Lavina said before she took a seat at the table.

"I could swear there were still a few more pieces," Elizabeth said, shaking her head when suddenly Bonny's cries reached them in the kitchen.

Lavina felt a smile curve her mouth as Elizabeth rushed towards Bonny's cries of distress.

A few moments later Elizabeth and Bonny carried in the large basket with eyes as wide as horse's hooves. "Lavina! Look! Someone left it on the porch!"

"Really?" Lavina asked pretending to be surprised. Tomorrow when she saw Eli, she would thank him for his generosity. She had no idea how he had managed to afford all the items in the basket, but she would be forever grateful to him.

"Here's a note," Elizabeth said pulling out a note stuck between a can of beans and a block of cheese. "*Gott has something great in your future. Isaiah 43:19.*"

"What's going on in here?" Johanna said walking into the kitchen, still wearing her robe.

"Look, Johanna. Someone left this for us on the porch!" Bonny exclaimed even as she began to unpack the basket.

As her sisters continued to chatter excitedly about how blessed they were by a Christmas angel sent by God, Lavina found herself captivated by the endless basket. It seemed as if Bonny would never stop reaching into the basket and coming up with more items they needed.

Finally, their kitchen table was stacked with anything and everything. There was rice, cheese, flour, sugar, and enough yeast to bake bread for a year. There were frozen meats, cleaning detergents, toiletries, and even toilet paper. There were even a few luxury items like candy, pretty candles, cookies, and canned fruits. Along with all the shop bought items there were even homemade items like jams, pickled vegetables, and mustards.

Lavina was dumbfounded, speechless, and completely baffled how Eli had managed to surprise them with such a generous gift. For a moment she considered telling her sisters it had been Eli's doing, but she decided against it.

He had delivered it at first light, when he'd expected everyone to still be fast asleep. If Lavina hadn't heard his footsteps in the snow, she wouldn't have even known that he was their mystery Christmas Angel, as Bonny had dubbed him.

Chapter 19
Hochmuth is a Sin

"Does this mean we can bake more cookies?" Daisy asked once the all the items had been put away.

Lavina couldn't remember the last time their pantry had been full. Just seeing all the shelves stocked with items that would last them two months or more, made it feel as if a weight had been lifted from her shoulders.

She wasn't sure how she could ever thank Eli for his generosity, but she knew that tomorrow, she would at least try.

She turned to Daisy and smiled. With two quilts ready to be sold and a full pantry, the least she could do was spend the day baking with her sisters. They hadn't made each other gifts this year and they couldn't afford to have their own Christmas feast, but they could abide by one tradition – baking cookies until all their tins were full.

"Of course we can, on one condition," Lavina said cocking a hand on her hip. "We bake a tin for the Smuckers as well. Our way of saying denke for being invited to Christmas lunch."

"And we're going to give Eli the Daisy I painted," Daisy quickly reminded her.

Lavina nodded. "Exactly. Now let's get the chores done, so the baking can begin!"

As soon as the younger girls left to do their chores, Johanna eyed Lavina with a curious look. "It wasn't you, was it? Lavina! You didn't sell the wedding ring quilt, did you?"

Lavina shook her head on a smile. "Nee, it's still safely tucked into the hope chest. It's like Bonny said, Gott sent a Christmas Angel to bless us with a full pantry."

Johanna looked at her suspiciously. "In that case I'm impressed that you allowed us to unpack it. You do know that Hochmuth is a sin."

Lavina frowned at her sister for a moment as she realized her sisters might have misunderstood her reasons for not wanting charity. "Johanna, do you think I'm too proud to accept charity?"

"Jah, what other reason could there possibly be for not wanting to go to the bishop? You and I both know the community will help us, if we ask…" Johanna pointed out.

Lavina shook her head. "I know that Johanna. But have you considered the Yoders, the Lapps, or even the Riehl family? The Yoders are broke ever since Mr. Yoder lost his job at the lumber factory. His whole family is depending on the community coffers now. Then there is the Lapps. Mrs. Lapp can't work and take care of her twins. Ever since Mr. Lapp passed away the community has been taking care of her as well. And as for the Riehl family, young Abram Riehl is fighting leukemia. His parents have been facing those medical bills for two years with no end in sight," Lavina explained. "It's not that I'm too proud to accept charity, I simply know that our community cannot afford to care for another familye now. If we accept anything from the community fund, that means less money for families that rely on it more."

Johanna let out a sigh. "Do you have to be so logical?"

"Jah. Because this is only temporary Johanna. As soon as we've paid off Mamm's medical bills we'll be back on our feet. We can be grateful for what we have, considering those families have even less. It's not because I'm too proud, it's because I don't want those families to suffer even more than they already do.""

Johanna nodded. "You're right. I didn't think of it like that."

"Exactly. And remember when Daed passed away? We lived off the community fund until I could begin to sell quilts."

"We did?" Johanna asked surprised.

"Jah, we did. Mamm and I didn't feel anyone else needed to know. The community fund has helped us through tough times in the past, but this time we need to find our own way out of our debt. We can't always turn to the community fund to throw us a rope," Lavina explained.

"You're a wise woman, schweschder." Johanna walked over and enveloped Lavina in a hug. When she stood back, she searched Lavina's gaze. "So, this basket didn't come from our community?"

"Nee," Lavina said firmly.

"Then from who?" Johanna asked, baffled.

"From a mystery Christmas angel." Lavina laughed, feeling happier than she had in months. "Kumm, let's start getting out the ingredients. I have a feeling we'll be baking the whole day if it's up to Bonny and Daisy."

"And we even got some chocolate chips in the basket, Bonny's favorite." Johanna retrieved the chocolate chips from the pantry. She shook her head on a smile. "May Gott bless our Christmas Angel and everyone and anyone that contributed to restocking our pantry. I swear I can look at it all day."

Lavina nodded with a smile. "I know, it's a great feeling, isn't it?"

With her heart light and happiness coursing through her veins, Lavina began to mix the first batch of cookies. She hadn't expected a miracle this Christmas, but now she knew that the basket of pantry goods hadn't been the miracle, it was meeting Eli Smucker.

Her heart swelled in her chest, wondering if he would ask her on a buggy ride again.

This time, she would say yes.

Chapter 20
A Flavor for Every Schweschder

On Christmas morning the excitement was tangible in the Schrock household as the sisters prepared to leave for the Smucker's.

Everyone had put on their Sunday best. Daisy was armed with the gift she had made for Eli and Bonny held the tin with a variety of cookies to thank the Smuckers for their hospitality. Everyone was excited, except for Lavina.

She couldn't help but feel nervous as she took the buggy's reins. After the rude way she had treated Eli the last time he had come by, she knew she owed him an apology. Then there was the basket with items for their pantry...she couldn't even begin to imagine how she could thank him for his generosity.

All her sisters were still in the dark about who had presented them with such a wonderful gift, and Lavina would keep it that way.

As they drove out of the yard, she realized Johanna had been right. If they hadn't been on their way to the Smucker home for Christmas lunch, their Christmas would've been a lot different. Even with a stocked pantry, Lavina knew that the day would've been overwhelmed by the absence of their mother.

Spending the day in a different community, in a different house, was exactly what her sisters needed to experience the magic of Christmas. They didn't need another reminder of losing their mother.

With the directions carefully explained on the Christmas card, Lavina found the Smucker farm without any trouble at all. The homestead was surrounded by large fields covered in snow. In the distance she could see almost like a tiny forest growing against the slope of a hill. Douglas Firs in different stages of growth could easily be spotted as she pulled into the yard.

She didn't know why she was surprised, but she hadn't expected the Smucker farm to be this big.

"Look at the trees. Are all of them Christmas trees?" Bonny asked eagerly, craning her neck out of the buggy to see.

"Jah." Johanna nodded.

"Even the small ones?" Bonny asked, surprised.

"Nee, Bonny. They still must grow before they'll be Christmas trees," Johanna explained.

"It's like a Christmas factory," Daisy said with wide-eyed admiration.

Lavina smiled at her sister's description. If only her sisters knew that this was where their mystery Christmas angel lived, on the farm that looked like a Christmas factory.

"Hullo! Merry Christmas!" a friendly woman called coming out of the house. She was a little older than Lavina's mother had been. She wasn't overweight, instead her features were merely softened with extra padding. Her eyes were kind, Lavina realized, as she stopped in front of the buggy. "I'm Ruth Smucker, and I am so happy you came!"

Lavina climbed out and walked to Ruth while her sisters followed. "Hullo Ruth, denke for the invitation. Merry Christmas to you too."

Once all the introductions were done, Ruth gestured for them to follow her into the house. "Eli and Daniel will join us shortly; they're just finishing up a few chores."

For a moment Lavina felt a little odd following Ruth inside, a woman they had just met.

As soon as they stepped into the house, that feeling faded. The Smucker home was welcoming and warm. A large Christmas tree stood by the fireplace with numerous gifts stacked below it. For a moment Lavina felt a twinge of regret that they hadn't done gifts this year.

"Who would like some cocoa? I already made it knowing you would be cold after travelling all this way," Ruth offered as she moved towards the kitchen.

Johanna laughed. "Everyone."

There was a pot simmering on the stove and potatoes waiting to be peeled. Lavina turned to Ruth with a smile. "Can I start peeling the potatoes for you?"

"Ach you don't have to do that, you're guests," Ruth insisted as she poured cocoa into five cups.

"I insist," Lavina offered picking up the paring knife. She had just begun when Eli stepped into the kitchen with a man that looked to be an older version of himself.

"You came," Eli said with a bright smile aimed directly at Lavina.

A blush colored her cheeks. "Merry Christmas, Eli."

"Merry Christmas to you all. This is my daed, Daniel," Eli introduced his father while his mother filled more cups with hot cocoa.

Once the introductions had been done for a second time, Ruth clapped her hands. "All of you go and sit by the fire, Lavina and I will finish up in here."

A short while later, Lavina couldn't help but be surprised how comfortable she felt working side-by-side with Ruth in the kitchen. Ruth was welcoming and warm and made it very clear that she was overjoyed to have a full table for Christmas lunch.

By the time lunch was finished and everyone took their seats at the table, everyone was in good spirits. Lavina expected Daniel to say a Christmas prayer. Instead Daniel jumped up and began to hand out the gifts from under the Christmas tree.

"You really didn't have to get us gifts," Lavina said feeling horrible that they hadn't brought something for the Smuckers.

"We wanted to," Ruth shrugged. "Besides, it's homemade. I've never had any dochders, so it was fun for me to get to spoil the lot of you."

"I made you something, Eli," Daisy said, pulling the ornament out of her pocket.

Lavina smiled, realizing her youngest sister had all but forgotten about her gift.

"I forgot the cookies in the buggy," Bonny was out of her chair and through the door before anyone could stop her.

Eli accepted the ornament with a big smile. Ruth gasped with adoration.

"This is special, Daisy. I'll hang it on the tree right now." Eli did as he promised.

When he returned to the table Daisy was beaming. "Now you can always remember the Schrock sisters."

"And Daisy in particular," Ruth added with a warm smile.

"Ach look, it's bath salts," Elizabeth exclaimed as she looked down at the gift she had unwrapped.

"Jah, I make them myself. I made a different scent for each of you. Lavina, you have lavender. Johanna, you have rose. Elizabeth, for you I made gardenia. Bonny, you have lily and lemon and for you Daisy, I made a scent you'll never guess?" Ruth wriggled her eyebrows.

"Chocolate?" Daisy asked hopefully making everyone laugh.

"Close, cherry," Ruth laughed.

The rest of the meal was just as wonderful as the Smuckers were welcoming. The food was delightful and the dessert, the best Lavina had ever tasted. When the meal was finished, Lavina stood up and began to gather the plates.

"Nee, leave them be. Take a walk with me?" Eli asked her in front of everyone.

For a moment Lavina felt a little embarrassed that he would ask her so openly. But as six pairs of eyes looked at her, almost encouraging her to agree, she finally nodded before turning to Johanna. "Could you and the girls please clear the table and wash up?"

"It's not necessary," Ruth insisted.

"It is," Johanna argued. "You've been so gut to invite us and give us gifts and spoil us with a wunderbar meal, we'll make sure you have no clearing up to do at all."

Ruth smiled warmly around the table before she rested her gaze on Lavina. "Your mamm would've been very proud of all of you girls."

The moment was heavy but brought a smile to every sister's face.

Lavina turned to Eli and drew in a sharp breath. "Let's take that walk."

Chapter 21
Cocoa and Promises

Lavina wasn't sure where they were going, as she followed Eli around the porch towards the barn. When he continued past the barn into a snowy field, she drew in a deep breath, savoring the clean air.

So far neither of them had said a word. Lavina wasn't sure if he was waiting until they were out of earshot or out of sight. But she didn't mind. For a moment, she just savored having spent a wonderful Christmas and now having Eli by her side to thank for it.

"You really made Mamm's day," Eli finally broke the silence. "She enjoys company, especially the company of women since it's usually just me and Daed."

"Your mamm and your daed are wunderbar Eli. You're so blessed to have such wunderbar parents." Lavina meant it with every ounce of her heart.

"Just like your schweschders are blessed to have you and you are all blessed to have each other." Eli stopped and turned to her. "I'm glad you came, Lavina. I've been looking forward to seeing you again."

Lavina smiled shyly and shook her head. "I can't see why? Ever since you met me you've done nothing but rescue me and my familye. I'd think we've become a burden."

"Not at all," Eli insisted. "It's been a privilege to help where I can."

"And the basket? That must have cost so much, Eli, denke so much. I haven't told the schweschders it was you, but I'd like to repay you for everything... in time."

Eli shook his head. "Repay me? Don't even consider it. When I told Mamm about your medical bills and wanting to help, she grabbed the reins from me and began a food drive in our community. We've been blessed with gut harvests this year; everyone was only glad that they could help."

"It wasn't you? Your community gave us all that food?" Lavina asked surprised.

"Jah. I just delivered it. I knew you wouldn't accept it if I showed up at your door, so I wanted to leave it on the porch... then you saw me..." Eli shrugged. "I'm glad you didn't return it."

"I couldn't." Lavina sighed. "It was wunderbar for the schweschders. Daisy dubbed you our mystery Christmas angel."

Eli chuckled. "I like the sound of that."

"Denke Eli. For the tree, the help, the delivery of the basket, for today, the gifts... I know denke will never be enough, but I mean it from the bottom of my heart. This Christmas would've much different if it hadn't been for you." Lavina held his gaze, hoping he could see the sincerity in her eyes.

Eli smiled and reached for her hands. "My Christmas would've been very different if it hadn't been for you. Just meeting you gave my Christmas meaning. Having all of you here today made me think of future Christmases. It would be lovely to have your familye at our table every year."

Lavina frowned curiously. "Eli, I already told you. Courtship just isn't possible now. I have Bonny and Daisy to think of."

"Your schweschders will always be part of your life Lavina. I'm not asking you to choose. I'm simply asking you to follow your heart. If it leads to a future with me, then I can't wait to help you raise Bonny and Daisy. You're more because of them, remember that," Eli insisted as he held her gaze.

Lavina's heart skipped a beat even as tears welled in her eyes. "Do you really mean that? You won't mind having two young girls? I can't just kick them out when they're baptized, Eli. They're my responsibility."

"And they'll be mine," Eli insisted before laughter bubbled from his throat. "Lavina, stop fighting against this. I know you enjoyed our buggy ride. I also know that you spent the next few days thinking of all the reasons that I shouldn't court you. How about I give you one reason why you should?"

All the defenses Lavina had built up since their last buggy ride were crumbling around her. Brick by brick she felt them fall, feeling her heart expand as Eli's warm hands held hers. "Why?"

"Because I've never felt this way before," Eli said earnestly. "Go on a buggy ride with me Lavina? One more buggy ride, one where you forget all those reasons you've thought of. A buggy ride where you allow yourself to think of the future. If at the end of that buggy ride, you can't see me in your future, I promise never to bother you again." Eli's eyes held hers.

Lavina felt her heart expand a little more. She had asked the Lord to guide her through her challenges, in answer the Lord had sent Eli to make their Christmas better. How could she deny Eli's request, when she already knew that the Lord had more plans for them?

Plans beyond Christmas.

Plans for the future.

She could feel it in her heart. She could see it in Eli's gaze.

A smile curved her mouth as she squeezed his hands. "I'm free tomorrow afternoon."

Eli's laughter flowed over her as he pulled her in for a hug. When he finally stepped back, his eyes glittered with hope. "I'll pick you up at noon. Dress warmly, it might take a while."

Hand in hand they returned to the house, only to see all four of Lavina's sisters watching them through the window, joined by Eli's mother.

Lavina turned to Eli with smile and shook her head. "I guess keeping this courtship a secret is going to be impossible."

Eli nodded. "Pretty much."

Their laughter blended in the cool afternoon air as they stepped onto the porch. The scent of freshly brewed cocoa hung in the air, a scent Lavina knew she would forever associate with Christmas and holding Eli's hand.

Chapter 22
A Romance Unfolds

Lavina wore her thickest coat as she walked to the buggy. She had a blanket tucked beneath her arm, wanting to make sure that it wasn't the cold that brought their buggy ride to an early end.

"I was afraid you might have changed your mind," Eli said as he took the blanket from her.

Lavina shook her head. "Even if I wanted to, my schweschders wouldn't have allowed it. Besides, I've been looking forward to our buggy ride all morning."

Eli's eyes widened with pleasant surprise. "That's gut news. I have a feeling today might be even more special than Christmas day had been."

Lavina laughed as she settled in the buggy. On the back seat there was a picnic basket which brought a frown to her face. "We're going on a picnic?"

Eli shook his head as he took the reins. "Not at all, but I thought a little of Mamm's cocoa might keep us warm, along with some leftover apple pie and sandwiches."

"That sounds like a picnic," Lavina smiled at him with a cocked brow.

Eli shrugged. "A buggy picnic then."

He called to the horse to step up, before he steered them out of the yard. With all four her sisters watching from the living room window, Lavina waved to them as Eli turned onto the dirt road.

Unlike with their last buggy ride, Lavina didn't feel nervous, or as if she had been forced into something she wasn't sure of. Instead, she found herself relaxing beside Eli, enjoying that he didn't always feel the need to fill the silence with mindless chatter. When he spoke, it mattered.

They drove until they reached a T-junction. Eli turned to her with a challenging grin. "Left, or right?"

Lavina laughed. "Right. I've never gone right before."

"Right it is," Eli agreed.

Soon the houses began to become further and further apart as they headed towards a forest in the distance. Eli pulled over on the side of the dirt road and reached into the back for the basket.

"Cocoa?"

"Jah, denke," Lavina said gratefully. She hadn't realized how cold it would be in the buggy. She laid the blanket over her knees and accepted the cocoa with a grateful smile.

"So as this is our first official buggy ride, I think there are quite a few things we need to talk about." Eli's tone of voice was foreboding, as if the *things* they needed to talk about weren't good.

"Like?" Lavina asked cautiously.

"Like would you like to have your own kinner one day? I've always wanted to have kinner, a whole house full of them. My parents couldn't have any more after me, but I've always wished to have a sibling. Seeing the way you are with your schweschders only makes me want a house full of kinner even more."

Lavina almost coughed as she took her first sip of cocoa. The last thing she had expected Eli to talk about this buggy ride, was her dreams for the future. "I uh...."

"It's alright," Eli insisted. "Take your time."

Lavina took another sip of cocoa before she answered. She wondered if Ruth would give her the recipe. "Kinner, jah. I've always dreamed of having kinner, at least three but hopefully five. I even quilted an heirloom quilt for my firstborn's cot."

"You did?" Eli asked impressed. "I'd like to see it some time."

Lavina sighed. "I had to sell it."

"I'm sorry to hear that, you'll just have to make another then," Eli said simply. "Next question, are there any chores you simply despise? That you'll want your mann to take over one day?"

Lavina laughed. "Splitting wood. And you?"

"Not really, although I'd prefer not to dry the dishes. I don't mind washing them, but I hate drying them," Eli shrugged.

"My turn for a question," Lavina said, meeting him with a challenging look. "Would you be willing to move to a different congregation?"

Eli thought for a long moment. Lavina couldn't help but fear that he wouldn't be willing. She wasn't sure she wanted to uproot her younger sisters if she and Eli married one day.

"I wouldn't mind moving to your congregation and living in the haus you were raised in, but I do have my daed's farm to think of. Do you think your schweschders would be excited about moving?" Eli asked.

Lavina sighed with a shrug. "I don't know. I can't imagine they'd want to leave all this behind."

"Then when the time comes, we let them decide," Eli said simply. "I can drive back and forth if they don't want to move."

Lavina shook her head. "You do realize you're talking about where we're going to live when we're married—we're not even engaged yet?"

Eli laughed. "Right, I probably should've started with that."

He climbed out of the buggy and Lavina watched him move around the buggy, wondering what he was up to. The last thing she expected was for Eli to kneel in front of her side of the buggy.

"I don't know everything about you, Lavina. But I know this. I know that you make my heart swell with affection. I know that you're kind, and generous, and friendly, and firm. I also know that I've never felt this way. When I look at you, I don't just see a woman or a schweschder... I see my future frau, I see the mamm of my kinner, I see my future. I'm sure we'll argue, I'm sure you'll get tired of me wanting to take care of you, and I'm sure I'll probably get tired of your stubbornness, but I'm also sure that together we can face any challenge. Will you do me the honor of accepting my hand marriage?" Eli held her gaze with a smile and a hand waiting for her to accept it.

Lavina's heart skipped a beat. For a moment a million thoughts raced through her mind. It was too soon. She hardly knew him. She couldn't just get engaged without consulting her sisters. She couldn't just think of her own future.

Johanna's words came to mind and Lavina felt a smile curve her mouth as calm and peace settled over her shoulders like a warm blanket.

"Jah, I'll marry you," Lavina said taking Eli's hand and stepping down from the buggy. "But not right away. I want a spring wedding; can you wait until then?"

Eli's laughter made her heart swell with love. "For you I'll wait until next fall, but spring does have a nice ring to it."

This time when Eli embraced her, Lavina knew that she wasn't being selfish. Embracing her own dreams and her own future was setting an example for her sisters.

That even when you face the biggest challenge of your life, love might come knocking unexpectedly.

Epilogue

Just like the year before, the house was filled with the scent of cocoa. The Christmas tree stood beside the fireplace, where flames were happily crackling in the hearth. Right front and center hung Daisy's ornament from the year before.

Lavina felt a smile curve her mouth. So much had happened between their first visit to Smucker farm last year, and today.

Christmas a year later.

"Lavina, please tell me Daisy and Bonny are staying home tonight. I can't believe how empty the farm feels when they go to visit Johanna and Elizabeth," Ruth said, coming out of the kitchen with a mug of cocoa.

"Jah, they're staying home tonight," Lavina nodded as she took a seat by the window.

From the living room window, she could see her new home. The home that Eli and Daniel had built for them in February. Lavina had been more than a little surprised by the choice Daisy and Bonny had made.

When they had told her schweschders about their engagement, Bonny and Daisy had leaped at the opportunity of moving to the Smucker farm and a brand-new house. Elizabeth and Johanna had been overjoyed at the news of

Lavina's engagement and had even surprised her by quilting a new heirloom quilt for her first born.

After the wedding, Lavina, Daisy, and Bonny had moved into the new house on the Smucker farm. Their presence was embraced just like it had been on their first visit. Daisy and Bonny now attended school in Eli's community but went to visit Johanna and Elizabeth most weekends.

Although Lavina and her sisters were still as close as they could be, it warmed Lavina's heart to know that both Elizabeth and Johanna were being courted. Just like Lavina had embraced her own happiness and her future, her sisters were embracing theirs now.

She could still remember how heavily her mother's debts had weighed on her shoulders last Christmas. They had finally managed to pay off all the debts before their pantry needed restocking after being filled by the charity basket from Eli's community.

Just like many things had changed since the year before, Lavina had learned so many lessons.

She had learned that her husband was truly an angel. One that treated her with love and respect and helped her raise her sisters as if they were his own siblings. She had also learned that prayers were answered, and that love came unexpectedly.

The last thing she had expected last Christmas was to fall in love.

And now, here she was a year later, happily married and settled into life on the Smucker farm. She still quilted for the farm stall, but Eli insisted the money she earned from her quilting should be saved for Bonny and Daisy's future, while he took care of all their household expenses.

"There you are," Eli said joining Lavina and his mother in the living room. "When I couldn't find you in the haus, I got a fright."

Lavina laughed and shook her head. "Could you please stop fussing, I'm fine."

Ruth joined in the laughter. "His daed was just like that. Fussed night and day until he held Eli in his arms."

"I'm not fussing, I'm merely concerned. You are growing another person. I can't begin to imagine how much strain that is putting on your body," Eli said concerned.

"Nothing a woman's body can't handle," Lavina assured him with a warm smile as she laid a hand over her swollen belly. "Only a few more weeks and you get to hold your boppli."

"Tomorrow we're going to finish the nursery," Ruth promised excitedly. "Daniel brought down Eli's crib from the hayloft yesterday."

Lavina smiled. She would leave the crib that had been used by her and her sisters, for one of her sisters to use. Using the Smucker family crib was important to Ruth. Considering how wonderful Ruth had been during her pregnancy, Lavina didn't mind giving in to one of her requests.

Just like her mother had been, Ruth had become more like a best friend than a mother-in-law.

"Here they are!" Eli cried out excitedly as a buggy pulled into the yard.

Lavina laughed. Just like Ruth missed Bonny and Daisy when they weren't home, Eli missed them as well. She couldn't help but be grateful for this family Gott had blessed her with. A family that had embraced her family as their own.

"Hullo Lavina, hullo boppli," Daisy said as soon as she reached Lavina. She pressed a kiss to Lavina's belly, clearly excited about the arrival of a new baby.

"Johanna's got news!" Bonny announced walking into the living room, her hands filled with gifts. She set the gifts down beneath the tree and Lavina's heart swelled with joy. Last year they couldn't even afford to give each other a gift and now they could afford gifts for the Smuckers.

"Merry Christmas," Elizabeth followed Bonny and set down more gifts. "These are for the boppli."

"Hullo, Merry Christmas," Johanna said, joining them in the living room.

"You have news?" Ruth asked eagerly.

Johanna nodded and even before she spoke, Lavina recognized the look in her sister's gaze.

"I'm engaged!" Johanna cried out excitedly. "He asked me last night, my very own Christmas miracle. We want to have the wedding in February. Ach, I'm just so happy!"

Lavina stood up and walked over to her sister. She framed Johanna's face and smiled into her sister's gaze. "I'm so happy for you. You deserve every happiness in the world."

Johanna stepped back, horrified, and for a moment Lavina thought she'd said something wrong when Johanna frowned at the pool of water at Lavina's feet.

Ruth's laughter made a very confused Lavina turn to her mother-in-law. "It was an accident."

"Jah, Lavina. It was an accident; your water just broke. I guess we're going to be blessed with another Christmas miracle, a boppli."

Lavina turned and met her husband's gaze with excitement.

She knew she was loved, supported and blessed.

*** The End ***

Thank you kindly for choosing to read my book. I sincerely hope you enjoyed it. All of my Amish Romances are wholesome stories suitable for all to enjoy.